Tropical Depression

a novel

Anne Russell

Bradley Creek Press

602 Bradley Creek Point
Wilmington, North Carolina 28403
910-256-3457

copyright 2013 Anne Russell
ISBN 978-0-615-87015-1

Cover design Cissy Russell

ALSO BY ANNE RUSSELL

~books~
The Wayward Girls of Samarcand
Wilmington A Pictorial History
Carolina Yacht Club Chronicles
Portraits of Faith
Seabiscuit Wild Pony of the Outer Banks
Wrightsville Beach Sketches
Waystations

~plays~
The Porch
The Coldest Night in Georgia
No More Sorrow to Arise
Dickens on the Rocks with A Twist
Scheme Dreamer
Emmaline
Ruckus
Dearly Beloved
Good Eats

~columns~
Goings-On

~documentaries~
Remarkable Journey The Cape Fear
Remarkable Journey The Albemarle
The Talented Tenth

Anne Russell has been entertainment editor and columnist for the Raleigh News & Observer, director of the arts for the City of Raleigh, and UNC professor of journalism and communications with MFA in Creative Writing and PhD in American Studies.

I will tell you it has taken me all my life to learn

that the line I call the horizon does not exist, and

sky and water, so long apart, are the same state

of being. I will not return to a universe of objects

that don't know each other. The world is flux, and

light becomes what it touches.

Monet Refuses the Operation

Leisel Mueller

Blues

When surf-casting for blues, bear in mind

these feeding fish can be aggressive to

swimmers in shallow water. Keep well

to the left or right of the swimming area.

Rule 47

Fearrington Yacht Club Handbook

Two. Four. Six. Eight. Dan McInnes took count of the pelicans riding the jade-green sea. Ten. Twelve. Fourteen. He always counted them in pairs, whether or not they came in matched sets. The blues were down now, but soon they would come up. The pelicans would rise in a body, dive, and lift off one by one against the cobalt sky, pouches heavy with menhaden chased by predatory blues.

He stepped forward and flung his line into the barely-rippling surf. It was a perfect day. White triangles moved separately against the horizon, and a freighter disappeared over the edge of the world. As a boy he feared the curved demarcation between sky and sea, imagining broken ships crushed in the abyss beyond the limits of his visual universe. In time he learned the optical illusion, but fear stayed with him. He trusted what he could see, and preferred not to test the hidden world. Like his father and grandfather before him, he had lived his entire life in Fearrington, with a break for college and law school.

Everything he needed was here, where time was measured by the tides. Why risk the unknown?

But he was no longer content. Something unquiet was going on inside him. Each September he gloried in the calm and clarity of Indian summer, absorbing it into his bones before winter closed in. Tourists gone, sea sparkled, breeze light against his cheek. No one else was aware of It, but he owned this place. It belonged to him. He had staked it out long ago, and he loved it. When his time came, he wanted his ashes scattered here, with a brace of bagpipes moaning a dirge.

He checked his other line, setting the rod more firmly in its spike. Nothing. Blues still down. Goddammit, be patient, old boy, they'll be up soon. What's your problem? Blues always come up. Perhaps it was his hormones. Last week he'd read somewhere that a man's hormones peak in early autumn after a summer buildup. He'd thought spring was the hormonal surge, so he'd arranged his tomcatting to coincide with the first blooms. But now he knew different and was having fantasies which used to form only in April. Must be power of suggestion. In August he'd turned sixty-six; his hormones couldn't still be strong. But on Tuesday—or was it Wednesday—he'd had a definite erection, when a thong-divided set of buttocks hove into view. Down, boy, he'd whispered to his nether region congested with desire. That gal could be your daughter. For shame!

He'd done without sex for months now. Or was it years? He hardly missed the act. The sex thing had somehow disappeared over the middle-age horizon. His wife didn't come on to him any more with her semi-monthly twitchings, and he'd quit chasing strange tail. Too goddamn much trouble. Too much guilt. He'd been married too long. His flirtation skills had become rusty. Suppose he caught a piece of tail? Perhaps he wouldn't be able to get it up, bingo! on demand, for whatever pussy happened to scout his neighborhood. What if he tried and failed? He'd do double-guilt, first for cheating on his long-suffering wife, and then for disappointing his lover. Easier to finesse it. No fuss, no muss, no bother. Rest on his laurels. Go quietly into his retirement. Go fishing instead.

The pelicans lifted and poised to dive. Bingo! Blues were up. Silvery finger mullet thronged the water. A long slow wave rolled across the sandbar. For a split second he glimpsed the procession of blues in its translucent crest. He felt his line go taut. Gotcha! Come home to Papa. His rod dipped as he began to play his catch. Easy now. Don't be too needy. He remembered his father's instructions: Landing a blue is like courting a cantankerous woman. Let him have his head. Play him gently at first. Tease him with the bait. Come here, go away. Make him hunger for it, fight to get it. Then when he thinks he's in control, set the hook and reel him in. His father referred to blues as "he." Cantankerous women were exciting when they were aggressive, his father said, and advocated making them more so. Yet Dan Sr. called blues "he." What was it all about? Was it the hormonal confusion of his father's declining years? His father's reasoning always defied the laws of logic, so Dan simply took his advice on faith, calling blues "he" but playing them like potential lovers. With a snap of the wrist he set the hook. Suddenly a Hobie cut across the water on a starboard tack. A jet-ski appeared to be chasing the Hobie, arrowing landward. A second jet-ski hovered nearby. Wave action propelled the Hobie into his line, and the cat-boat capsized into the surf. Damn! He'd lost his blue. Oh well. There'd be another, if his rig hadn't been cut.

The Hobie drifted in the lee of the bar. A sleek head bobbed to the surface and a trim form scrambled to right the boat. He squinted at the scarlet-clad bottom wriggling and squirming. Well-tanned thighs dangled over the edge of the canvas. He didn't recognize the bottom. Probably not a Club member. A member would know better than to sail a Hobie into fisherman territory. But the bottom caught his interest. Strange tail, and it wasn't half-bad. It knew all the moves. He hoped it belonged to a woman, because he'd hate to be excited by the buttocks of a boy. He'd heard that as men aged, sometimes they turned from women toward boys. That hormonal thing. When he was a teenager, an aging Club member had begun to eye him in the shower, hover around him at the snack bar. Dan had kept his distance, and sure enough, one day he heard the blue-haired ladies whispering in their rockers on the porch. The man was never seen again, banished to wherever they send people who offend Club sensibilities. Dan thought he caught sight of the man once up by the northern inlet, hanging around the dunes where condoms lay limp in the sand on Sunday mornings. But he couldn't be sure.

He heard a shout, and the scarlet bottom slipped back into the surf. The Hobie caught a whiff of wind and headed over the bar. The sleek head moved shoreward, tan shoulders emerged, and a red bikini top appeared. The sailor was a female. Thank god! A stream of profanity accompanied her rapid exit from the water. She couldn't possibly be a Club member, not with that mouth. "Shit!" he heard her say. "Shit! Goddamn!" She limped, bending toward her right ankle. My god, she took my hook. That'll teach her. He stuck his rod into the other spike and waded out to offer her a hand as she set her bare feet on the broken shells roiling at the tide's edge.

Sinking onto the beach, she touched her fingers to her ankle. "Sonofabitch bit me." She held her fingers up for him to see. They glistened red, and a thin red ooze snaked toward her heel.

"Musta been a sand shark."

She flung back, "I thought those itty-bitty sharks weren't supposed to bite."

He wiped his hand on his shirt and pressed his palm against the wound above the silver trinket encircling her ankle. "Bluefish," he said. "Mean as the devil. See that leg bracelet you're wearing? How it sparkles in the sun? That's what attracted Mr. Bluefish. Blues'll go for anything bright and shiny. Don't need bait to catch 'em. Just a shiny lure. Bent spoon'll do the trick." As he inspected the teeth marks on her ankle, he caught himself glancing sideways toward the apex of her inner thighs. Dammit, Dan, that's forbidden territory. A decent man doesn't conduct search and destroy missions in those waters. He

10

ought to be ashamed of himself. But he couldn't help noticing the inviting swell of—what was that euphemism?—her bermuda triangle.

She surely wasn't a Club member, so it couldn't be too much of a sin to steal one peek. He'd learned in adolescence not to lust too strongly after the daughters of Club members. For one thing, they might be his second or third cousins, and for another, they pretended to be nice girls. Non-members, on the other hand, were fair game. He could slouch anonymously in the shadow of the lifeguard stand and fantasize about them to his heart's content, allowing his lewd thoughts to trail them up the beach as their breasts danced a jig. He imagined passionate embraces in the lee of the jetties. He licked his lips as if receiving salty tongue-kisses. Their buttocks swayed, and his groin ached for sandy thrustings as waves beat upon the shore.

"My boat! It's going out to sea!" The woman's words snapped him back to the present. In tandem, the two jet-skis veered toward shore, making action which propelled the disabled Hobie seaward. It gathered speed as it filliped in the surf.

"Damn nautical gnats," said Dan. "I hate the blasted things. No respect for marsh-life, make godawful noise. We need an ordinance to ban them." The woman struggled to rise. "Don't you go back into the water until the bleeding's stopped. Bluefish'll get blood lust. I'll bring your Hobie in for you."

He took after the errant catamaran, stroking furiously with the current, wishing he hadn't let himself get so out of shape. Not many years before, he'd been a sea creature, able to swim tirelessly, ride wave after wave. That was before the thing happened to his son, when the sea became his enemy rather than his friend. Now he noticed a drag as he kicked his legs. Was he caught in a sudden riptide? He was wearing bermuda shorts, and also had on a shirt. What a ridiculous Galahad he must seem, floundering fully clothed. As he struggled toward the Hobie, the sodden fabric dragging him down, the jet-skis taunted him, soaring into the air as the waves crested, dropping back into the water, making circles around him, sending up plumes of foam. The two young men at the controls laughed at his plight. He raised his arm and gave them the high-sign, though the effort caused him to gulp a mouthful of sea water. I hate you bastards, he thought, I hope you break your stupid, arrogant young necks. As soon as the murderous wish came into his consciousness, he felt a twinge from some private place in his soul, and he reconsidered. Why was he trying so hard to play the role of hero for this strange woman? If he let nature take its course, the Hobie would drift with the current and beach itself somewhere south of the fishing pier.

Turning shoreward, he scanned the line of beach from pier to pier, estimating the time it would take for the Hobie to find its way into shallow water. The woman in the red swimsuit waved at him from her vantage point beside his fishing rod. The long sweep of sand spread out on either side of her, stretching toward the northern and southern inlets which governed the waters of the sound. Behind her was the low ridge of dunes which partially obscured the double rows of shingled cottages. The Fearrington Yacht Club sat squarely in the middle of the island, its wide porches and annexes occupying more beachfront than any other structure. Founded more than a century earlier by a group of competing yachtsmen related through blood or marriage, over the decades the Club had become extended family numbering upwards of five hundred members. Each spring a handful of direct descendants was voted into membership through secret ballot, and a new season was begun.

A boardwalk led from the center of the Club through the dunes onto the beach. At the end of the boardwalk a sturdy lifeguard stand rose twenty feet into the air. In its left corner a flag pole announced the condition of the surf. A green flag indicated all was well. When waves were choppy or a strong current ran along the sidebar, a yellow flag warned swimmers to proceed with caution. When a rip current, northeaster, or hurricane made swimming a matter of life and death, a red flag served as the keep-out sign. And when the lifeguard was not on duty, a black flag signalled swimmers they were on their own. On this flawless early-autumn day, a green flag ruffled in the breeze. Waving back at the woman who lost control of her Hobie, Dan flopped onto his back and closed his eyes, giving himself over to the tug of the current. Inhaling deeply to fill his lungs, he floated in the cool brine like a large jellyfish. He dangled in the green suspension, arms and legs washing to and fro like the tentacles of a man-o'-war. He licked his sunburned lips where sea-salt had puckered them. Water filled his ears, blotting out all sound except the whine of the jet-skis. He opened his eyes, winced at the seawater's sting. Blue sky blurred through radiance of sunlight. White clouds sailed far above him. He lost his sense of time and place. The woman on the beach, the errant Hobie, his fishing tackle, his obligations to his wife Nora dissolved into the amniotic fluid surrounding him. He was again in his mother's womb, a helpless thing, amorphous, free of obligation, waiting to be born. What was it he learned in grade school? The salt content of human blood approximates that of the oceans. He was part of the sea, the sky, the bluefish, the pelicans, lost in infinity. Could drowning be like this, a letting go, a conscious giving over to forces beyond this mortal coil? A sense of peace came over him. He would let the tide take him to wherever the Hobie drifted, and he would pull the boat onto the sand until its hapless sailor could reclaim it. Let the young fools on jet-skis have their fun chasing each other in their noisy water-chariots, the rush of wind in their faces, their hearts pounding. They'd only be young once. So soon the stillness comes.

"Hey, Nora, honey. You doin' good?"

Nora McInnes shoved items deep into the cypress-wood locker and slammed the door shut before turning to face the curious eyes of the sun-reddened bleached blonde who stepped from the shower stall onto the boards of the ladies' dressing room. Water dripped off the blonde's pudgy, freckled body and ran through slats onto the sand below.

"I'm fine, Jerianne," Nora trilled. "How 'bout you?"

Jerianne stared at the numerals on Nora's locker. "Why, that's number 73, honey. You sure you're in the right place? I coulda sworn you had locker 14, around the corner."

Nora hated Jerianne, with her brassy hair and stretch marks and pendulous breasts resting on her bloated abdomen. Obviously pregnant again. Weren't four little Eldridges enough? Must Jerianne bring one more into the world for everyone else at the Club to discipline? No wonder Bill Eldridge had to fortify himself with increasing amounts of gin at the upstairs bar. Bedding the fertile Jerianne must be a daunting task for a man so shy he always looked down at his topsiders when speaking.

"Jussa minute, honey," said Jerianne. She waddled away, dabbing at her wet hair with a large towel imprinted with sea turtles, her wide white buttocks swaying. She disappeared around the far side of the lockers, returned holding a large carton of Kentucky Fried Chicken. "G'wan, have some," she said, thrusting the greasy chicken toward Nora. Nora shook her head negatively and pressed her

16

lips tightly together. "O, g'wan," insisted Jerianne. "You could eat this whole bucket and never show it, you're wasting away before our eyes."

"I have a personalized fitness program," replied Nora. "Diet, exercise, the whole works. No point letting myself get sloppy. I shouldn't have to mention it, but bringing food into the ladies' locker room is against Club rules. Attracts ants and roaches, you know."

Jerianne laughed heartily before retrieving her baggy, faded swimsuit from the shower and turning toward the dressing stalls. "Rules, schmools! If I didn't eat my way through my first four months, Bill couldn't live with me."

"I bet he couldn't," said Nora. She hastened into the nearest toilet stall and flushed the commode before sticking her forefinger down her throat and vomiting into the rushing water.

Dan stowed his fishing gear beneath the Club steps, washing off under the outside water spigot. He closed his eyes and bent forward so the cool fresh water poured over the nape of his neck and coursed down his adam's apple. Shaking his head from side to side, he straightened and squinted. The woman in the red bikini was making faces at him.

"I thought you were a gentleman," she teased. "Club rules say ladies first, don't they?" She ran her fingers through her sea-soaked long hair.

He was seized by an impulse he hadn't felt since he was a kid. "Sure do!" He gripped the spigot with his palm and aimed an arc of water toward the woman from the catamaran. She ducked to catch the water in her mouth as it splashed over her shoulders, then expertly spit it onto his chest, squatting like a little girl beneath the spigot.

"You gave up on my Hobie," she pouted, her wet lips glistening.

"Your Hobie's on the beach south of the fishing pier. Give me a whistle, and I'll help you retrieve it." Backing away, the woman put two fingers into her mouth and whistled. Water droplets flew in the bright sunshine as she ran up the boardwalk toward the ladies' annex. Dan grabbed a towel from the porch railing, caught her, and wrapped it around her. The moment his arms encircled the woman's shoulders, he saw Nora coming toward them. She had on one of the outfits she wore for bridge luncheons, and she did not appear to be pleased.

18

"My wife Nora," he said lamely, as Nora planted herself next to him.

The woman adjusted the towel about her body, tucking it in just above her left breast as if it were a sarong. She held out her thoroughly-washed right hand. "Hello. I'm Windham," she said, ignoring Nora's frown. "Windham Doubeck. Perhaps you know Clark Doubeck. He's my uncle."

Dan felt relieved. "Clark's your uncle? Imagine that! Imagine that, Nora. Her uncle's Clark Doubeck."

Nora stood straight as a mast in a sunset calm. "I heard her," she said archly.

"Why, Clark and I've sailed many a race together. Haven't we, Nora? Yessir, that Clark's taken the Commodore's Cup so often we're thinking of naming it the Doubeck Cup. Right, Nora?"

Nora was unmoved, arrayed in her blue-and-white-striped dress perfectly matching her belt adorned with signal flags. Dan moved closer to Nora, hoping to placate her by publicly affirming their partnership. "I'm Dan McInnes," he explained to Windham. "And she's Nora

McInnes." His still-damp arm brushed lightly against the sleeve of Nora's dress, causing her to pull away from him.

Finally Nora spoke in her carefully-modulated steel-magnolia voice. "Windham...Doubeck. How delightful to make your acquaintance. Are you on our guest register, or....?"

"I'm new," said Windham. "Granddaughter of a member. Legacy, I believe you call it. Used to come here when I was a kid. Nice to be back, after so long." Smiling, she headed for the ladies' dressing room. "I'm sure we'll meet again soon."

Nora made a half-turn to watch Windham cross the front porch. "No swimsuits allowed on the chair side of the white line," Nora called after her. "Always observe the white line."

Tucking the chamois into his front pocket, Dan admired his work. Good job! Nora's blue Buick sparkled in the sunlight. She was a stickler who would notice every water spot. He deserved a cold brew, or two or three. An afternoon of NFL reruns, settled into his comfortable ugly chair, feet up, a bowl of popcorn propped at his elbow. He surveyed his domain, his large brick colonial-style residence in the center of landscaped green. Azaleas and camellias bordered the yard, interspersed with hydrangea and forsythia, beneath huge live oaks draped in Spanish moss. Since he had inherited the house thirty years earlier, he had groomed it so well that each spring it was on the garden tour, debutantes in hoop-skirted Gone-With-the-Wind dresses gracing the front lawn. When he was appointed Chief Judge of the Superior Court, Nora insisted their place become at least as imposing as that of her best friend, the wife of the cardiovascular surgeon who excised Nora's varicose leg veins. She installed a lawn sprinkler system and meditation garden and had the McInnes coat-of-arms carved into the front door. The past two years, Dan hired a crew of Mexicans to groom the yard on Fridays, relieving his arthritic back from too much bending. He didn't care whether or not the Mexicans were illegals. In the years since the civil rights movement, black yard workers had become scarce, and spoiled white teenagers were loathe to mow lawns and bag up fallen magnolia leaves.

Halfway up the back steps, he remembered he was out of beer. Marty and Bill had drunk him dry the night before. He couldn't hightail it to the Town Mart until noon, in deference to Sunday blue law on alcohol sales. Damn stupid law. The Presbyterian and Episcopal churches served wine at their services, but the stores couldn't sell a drop. Perhaps that was the real motive behind the hypocrisy. Make all the dipsomaniacs attend church to feed their addiction on Sunday mornings, dropping tokens into the collection plate as payment for the Communion-rail dispensation. At court Dan always had a problem dispensing justice for violations of the "morality" laws, because of the several motes in his own eye. But he'd justified his guilty verdicts by telling himself the real crime was being stupid enough to get caught.

One case still bothered him. A local college professor, respected in the community for many years, had been snared during a periodic crackdown on prostitution in the public park. The poor fellow had been charged with offering to pay fifty dollars to give an undercover vice cop a blow job. Dan could hardly keep his face straight as he sat on the bench in his judicial robes. Imagine paying to give one, not get one! Perhaps the defendant was heeding the Biblical admonition 'tis more blessed to give than to receive. Dan managed to maintain his decorum in spite of the fact that he considered prostitution laws essentially unenforceable. Within days after a crackdown, the same

22

transvestites were plying the same street corners with the same degree of success. While personally repelled by the behavior, Dan had come to the conclusion that homosexuality shouldn't be against the law, so long as experienced in private with other consenting adults. Nevertheless, he convicted the prof based on the evidence, and the prof's life soon fell apart. His wife left him; he was fired from his tenured position for conduct unbecoming a faculty member. All because he sought to assuage a private need in a fee-for-service arrangement. But to Dan, in the final analysis, the prof deserved his punishment. He should've walked into any waterfront bar at closing time and found a horny seaman to cocksuck free of charge, or driven a half-hour up to the Marine base, where both male and female prostitution are considered a time-honored patriotic tradition necessary to the morale of fighting men and a flourishing local economy.

Every time his ruling in the prof's case troubled Dan, he soothed his own residual guilt with the belief that the greatest sin in these matters is gross indiscretion, embodied in the legendary quote, do what you will but don't do it in the street and frighten the horses. He applied this to heterosexuals as well as homosexuals. If you're going to have an extramarital romance, don't leave a paper trail. Indulge only in spoken words of endearment, no love letters; pay cash at the motel, no credit cards. When engaging in one or another of the human depravities, do it out of town, don't shit in your own back yard. This was polite society's unspoken creed. One ignored it at one's peril, committing contributory negligence or wilful misconduct.

Dan felt for his wallet in the back pocket of his trousers. Washing Nora's car in his good pants put his cash flow right at hand. But he'd left his car keys in the house, and he didn't feel like going back inside where Nora would shanghai him into attending church with her, a fate he would just as soon eschew. All his life he'd done the church thing in the proper evolutionary order: acolyte, crucifer, usher, vestry. But he'd increasingly found himself bored with Sunday-go-to-meetin.' He'd rather surf-cast or ocean-sail or sit and read a book on the Lord's Day. St. Philip's had seen a rapid succession of ministers in recent years, all good sorts, genuinely interested in their calling. Yet somehow each had managed to offend the ruling contingent of the congregation, and had duly been banished to another vineyard. Christ himself would have failed to meet the standards of St. Philip's, for Christ had been known to ruffle a few feathers among the establishment. The word had spread on the Episcopal grapevine about peevish St. Philip's, and each succeeding rector had been more homogenized than his predecessor, until Sunday service reached the ultimate socially-acceptable blandness.

As a member of the vestry, Dan annually followed tradition and put the current rector up for courtesy Yacht Club membership. On Saturday nights, he would see Reverend—what was this one's name?—Reverend Christopher Bradley III—Dan would see Reverend Bradley downing his share of Scotch at the Club bar and eating his fill on the communal dining porch, failing to note that the Club lacked the diversity Christ surely would have espoused, since the only non-white on Club premises was the handyman. Dan forgave himself for belonging to an all-white social club because he had paid his own entry fee to Heaven through dutiful years of church attendance at Episcopal St. Philip's, with polite attention to the gutless wonders who temporarily inhabited the pulpit. Surely at this stage of life, though political correctness dictated lip service bemoaning the failure of St. Philip's and the Yacht Club to racially integrate, God would understand Dan's need to relax and simply enjoy his retirement without leading the charge for diversity.

To hell with the car keys. Dan would walk to Town Mart. Burn up some time and maybe some calories. When he finally got to his destination, the blue law would be over, the beer case would be unlocked, and he'd've worked up a good thirst. A glance at the kitchen and bedroom windows reassured him Nora wasn't spying, and he took off down Ponciana Street.

The usual Sunday silence reigned, with an occasional car loading for the weekly pilgrimage to the church of its choosing. Dan turned at Magnolia and had no trouble crossing the boulevard because traffic was light. Backyard gardens were ramshackle, defeated by the scourge of relentless summer heat. House renovations in the adjacent blue-collar neighborhood had stepped up, probably because of gentrification taking advantage of low interest rates. Outside the city limits, the new-rich were building monster houses where they only paid county taxes until annexation was biting at their heels. Dan had never wanted a shiny new house with as-yet-unknown structural defects. He preferred to maintain the McInnes dwelling he'd always known, content himself with what he had. He pitied his friends who in midlife had gotten rid of aging wives and acquired trophy wives with higher maintenance.

Much smarter to pay for a spa and facelift for the mother of your children, tune her up for the sunset years.

As he walked, he could see the one-story bungalows along the old trolley line were moving up and out with enclosures and additions. Driveway densities had increased, either because more people could afford cars or because boomerang adult children had returned home. Change was in the air. Something was going on. Things weren't as they always had been, but he saw nothing startling. It was a time of transition, yet also of entrenchment. In Washington, the same-old same-old, outs seeking to banish ins, ins trying to stay in at all costs. Same old lies being told, same old tainted money changing hands. He wasn't sure why, but Harry Truman was the only President he had ever respected. Something about his lack of panache. He said what he meant, and what you saw was what you got. No surprises. Democratic rumor mill said a black Senator from Illinois was moving quickly onto the Presidential horizon, guy with a foreign name. Fat chance he would have to win the Presidency. If he were a black named Jack Morrison, well, maybe. Hillary Clinton had been angling to be the first female American President, and even with her Bill baggage, she would have

27

a better shot. Chicago ranked high on the corruption ladder. A black from Chicago wouldn't be good news.

Dan meant to take his customary dogleg to avoid the black neighborhood, but impulsively he walked straight ahead into long-forbidden territory. Growing up in Fearrington, he'd learned to heed invisible boundaries which delineated where and when nice people didn't go. Walk here, drive there, don't evereverever enter this place or that, stay in your place or else you'll deserve any bad consequences of breaching protocol. Lock your car on some streets, on others roll down your windows for fresh air. Take evening strolls down this street, avoid that one. Yet here he was violating his routine, compelled to explore that which heretofore had been invisible to him, as the boundaries fell away. The simple act of walking wherever he wished, following his own instincts, gave him a light and free feeling. His steps quickened and he breathed more easily. He felt as if he were in one of his flying dreams, floating effortlessly, burdens lifted, horizons unlimited, no longer shackled by gravity.

The houses on these narrow streets were a bit shabby but neater than he had imagined them to be. Yards were cared for, some with decorative cement figures or painted rocks lining front walks. Pots of flowers and well-used settees on porches. Here and there a window was open to the morning sunshine, and a cat arched its back on a railing. He could smell ham baking, chicken frying, Sunday dinner in progress. Aunt Sally's appeared in his mind, the venerable three-story house on Madeline Street, with all its porches. Sunday dinner at Aunt Sally's. What a treat! His uncles, cousins, grandparents, mother and father, brothers, and the occasional guest who wasn't quite family but almost. Migod, he loved his family! They had slowly disappeared, one by one over the years, slipped away when he wasn't looking. He would find himself in Oakview Cemetery on cold January days, among the ancient gravestones, staring at a new raw scar in the earth. He no longer had to make duty calls to the two nursing homes, one downtown and one way out on the beach road. The grand procession of McInneses had marched inexorably into the Mysterious Realm. Soon it would be his turn. He hadn't that many autumns, springs, summers, left. He made a silent vow not to die in January, the dreariest month. He would die after the azaleas had bloomed in springtime, or perhaps in October's bright blue weather.

Preoccupied with his thoughts, he stubbed his shoe on an uneven bit of sidewalk. Dammit, Dan, get off that maudlin train of thought. You're starting to hyperventilate.

You're still viable, old boy. You don't have cataracts. Or a hip implant. Or prostate cancer. You've your own hair. There's life still to be lived. Stop wallowing in the negative. Let it be!

He inhaled deeply. Some force tugged him farther and farther into this black neighborhood, around corners, across streets. Something more than idle curiosity. Something unfamiliar, a kind of vibration. He felt a pulsing, a throbbing. Then he heard it. A jingling, a jangling, a boom-de-boom. He rounded a corner, and there it was. A squat brick church, smack in the middle of the residential area, fronting on the one-way which knifed at a fast pace through the guts of the black district. He felt slightly disoriented. From the look of it, the church had been here all his life, yet he'd never known of its existence. Free Will Holiness read the neatly-lettered sign on the small square of lawn. Free Will. One of those black churches, like the AME Zion and the Jehovah's Witness and the Pentecostal. He'd never been able to distinguish among them. All he knew was they were black, he was white, and he had no interest in them. Live and let live.

Yet here he was, moving closer to the front steps, his legs propelling him without his brain directing. He checked his watch. Eleven-fifty. Church should be letting out

30

shortly. The sign read Sunday School 11, Morning Service 11:45. Different hours from mainstream white churches. Wonder why? Perhaps he should take a peek inside, a tiny peek. Through the crevice between the front doors. No one would see him. He must witness what created the jingling-jangling-booming sound. St. Philip's had only an organ, albeit a magnificent one imported from Switzerland, which had cost his family a hefty contribution. But St. Philip's organ made no such sound as this. He'd just slip inside for a moment, stand way at the back. Yet maybe he shouldn't. He wasn't wearing a jacket or tie. Was he presumptuous to come unbidden into the midst of the "other"? A white man without proper attire? T.S. Eliot buzzed in his brain. I grow old, I grow old, shall I wear my trousers rolled, shall I part my hair behind, do I dare to eat a peach? He patted his wallet for reassurance. A little something in the collection plate would show his respect. From the look of it, this church could use all the help it could get. Paint was peeling from the doors, front steps needed repair. His white man's dollars, freely given, would most likely be appreciated.

He gently pushed open the outer door to the church, passed quietly through the empty vestibule, and began to ease forward one of the inner doors. Suddenly the door swung away from him and he stood exposed at the end of the bright red aisle-runner which culminated at the pulpit. The smiling face of a teenaged black girl appeared from behind the door. She handed him a tambourine. Good God! He hadn't held a tambourine since kindergarten. What did she expect him to do with it? He dared not reject it, as if to appear ungrateful and hostile. He was stuck with it. He couldn't just duck in and out as he had intended. Every movement might produce a jingle or a jangle and cause heads to turn to witness his rapid exit. Nodding thanks, he headed for the empty back pew. "No, no," the girl whispered. "Sit up front where you can hear."

He could hear perfectly well. Hearing was what had brought him to this church in the first place. He didn't want to sit up near the front. But another smiling face, that of an aging woman in a spectacular go-to-church hat, beckoned him forward. She gestured toward the vacant space beside her and moved in a semi-crouch into the aisle to grant him passage. He had never seen such a hat, wrapped around her head in two contrasting bands of vibrant color, ascending heavenward like a steeple. Glancing around surreptitiously, he saw other extraordinary hats, dipping low, rising high, spreading outward. His spirits soared in the midst of the sassy chapeaux. Nothing

32

modest or humble here. The hats were brash, expressive, outward and visible signs of inner joy. And the red of the aisle-runner, unabashedly red, brilliant, not subdued like the burgundy runner in St. Philip's. Red like the Blood of the Lamb. Like the blood in his veins. Like the blood in the veins of this congregation. Like the blood snaking down Windham Doubeck's ankle. The blood of life. Red like the tip of a rutting dog's erect phallus. Good god! What was he thinking? His mind had taken off on its own lewd trip, beyond his censorship.

He clutched his loaned tambourine and mouthed the vaguely-familiar hymns with their unfamiliar cadences, slyly eyeing his fellow worshippers, expecting disapproval for his mangled attempts to make a joyful noise. "Dance, dance, wherever you may be...I am the Lord of the Dance, said He...," came from his throat with more force than he intended. He was the only white person among them, but no one paid him any mind. They didn't give a damn that he was an interloper. He was irrelevant to their world. They simply went on about their Sunday business.

As the heat of midday baked the church, religious fervor caused the temperature to rise in the nave, and handheld fans appeared stamped *Foster's Funeral Home,* fluttering in rhythm with the music. In the midst of life we are in

33

death, Dan mused. He didn't want to ruminate on death, but his mind was on its own trajectory. So live that when thy summons comes to join the innumerable caravan which moves to that mysterious realm where each shall take his chamber in the silent halls of death.... Why did they require students to memorize Thanatopsis when they are at life's threshold? He was now approaching life's exit, and he wanted to seize life while it was still within his grasp; he did not want to go gentle into that good night.

To the right of the pulpit, a handsome black man in a flashy suit commanded the singing, face lifted upward, eyes closed, fingers adorned with ornate rings whose stones scattered light. He gave the cues, set the pace, performed solos, toned it down, brought it back up. The congregation clapped its hands louder and louder. Foot-stomping began. Sedate matrons in pastel dresses shook ample buttocks, thighs, bosoms. A small boy stared in awe at his mother's quivering flesh beneath her layers of fabric. He circled his arms about her as far as they would go, and rode her dancing hips, up and down, around and around, forward and back. He was learning the primal motion, in celebration of the God who had brought him to life in his mother's womb.

One woman danced in her pew, arms heavenward. Other women twirled and gyrated with raised arms. The men thrust their arms toward the vaulted ceiling. Was this what it meant to Signify? Dan had heard that word from the black nannies and cooks and laundresses who were integral parts of his parents' and grandparents' households. He'd always wondered about Signify. Or perhaps this was what they meant by Praise. Praise the Lord. And pass the ammunition, he thought as he read the inscription above the chancel: No weapon that is formed against thee shall prosper. Isaiah 54:17. The Biblical quotation was punctuated with a sword.

A chill went over him. Beneath the warmth and celebration, a hostile undercurrent flowed. Was he the enemy? Of course he was. White people were the enemy. What was he doing here? How dare he invade black turf? This was their sacred gathering place, their haven, where they could gird themselves against white oppression. He searched the faces of the congregation, painfully aware of his pale face, and distinguished differences he had never before noticed. Rather than blending together in one dark-pigmented mass, each face became distinct. This one had high cheekbones, that one jowls, another a pointed chin, a

wide nose, a long nose.   Here onyx, there café au lais,
over there a sprinkling of freckles.

The church seemed charged with kinetic energy.   He
felt the power all around him.   Good god.   If this energy
were unleashed rather than held in check by the shackles
of religion, white people wouldn't stand a chance.   Oh
thank you, thank you, he groveled in his heart, thank you
for taking your frustrations to Christ and shaking
tambourines and singing praise songs, rather than smiting
us for our transgressions against you.   Thank you for
allowing me to come unto your table unbidden, for
accepting me rather than attacking me like a pack of
hungry wolves.   Oh thank you, dear Eliza, for doing our
laundry and gratefully receiving my mother's hand-me-
down coat which passed for your Christmas present.
Thank you for not washing our clothes in poison, for not
suffocating me as I slumbered in my crib.

The energy infected each worshipper to a fever pitch.
At first, Dan sat rigidly in the pew as he did at St. Philip's,
lip-synching the words to the hymns.   Now his larynx and
pharynx produced sound.   He jumped to his feet, joined in
the   hand-clapping   and   foot-stomping,   causing   his
tambourine to frantically jingle and jangle.   A few faces
turned in his direction, breaking into smiles.   He felt

absolutely wonderful moving in the Spirit. The constant ache in his arthritic neck had evaporated. This was fun! No wonder blacks came eagerly to church. The children weren't bored and fidgety like they were at St. Philip's during the "grownup" service. Here they were praising and stomping and clapping and shaking their child-sized tambourines. The church had become a living organism which thundered and shook, like a giant dinosaur come back to life.

What must this commotion sound like outdoors? The noise was so intense, surely it could not be contained within these four walls. It must be rumbling across the neighborhood into downtown, into the historic district, to the river's edge, a great rush of joyful noise. Every cell within him was vibrating, as if he had received electroshock therapy. He thought of the woman in the Hobie capsized in the breakers. Why had he not left his fishing rods and tackle on the beach, floated away with her on the tide, followed her scarlet bottom wherever it wriggled, through the inlet to Mason's Island, where they could lie naked on the beach and copulate in the dunes. What was he thinking of? He was In church, for God's sake, having lewd and lascivious thoughts. What was wrong with him? Everyone else was immersed in the love of the Lord, but he was caught up in lust for this woman made flesh. He should flee this primitive place, recover his civilized wits, buy his six-pack at Town Mart, go home and numb out with the NFL.

Just when he thought he would levitate, the door on the right marked Pastor burst open, and an enormous black man strode forth wearing a white robe, waving a white Bible, flashing a gold front tooth. He embodied every black-preacher stereotype of B-grade movies, and the faces of the congregation brightened with expectancy as their Reverend took possession of the throne-like wooden chair behind the pulpit. The preacher's great legs quivered, and he opened his trembling eyelids, leapt to his feet and seized the pulpit with both hands. "The Word is out!" he shouted. "The Word is out!"

The congregation echoed him. The Word is out! They turned toward each other conspiratorily. Dan hardly knew how to respond to the intense dark eyes next to him beneath the amazing hat. Am I the only white person to know the Word is out? Is the Word out that I'm over here finding out that the Word is out? Should I tell my friends the Word is out? He felt his lifelong sense of white superiority and entitlement drain through his feet into the floorboards as he realized the preacher was a master psychologist, the black incarnation of Jesus. His implicit message was clear: We have aught to fear but fear itself. The conspiracy of silence is broken. The Word is out that White power is merely an illusion, and Black power, held in check for so many generations, will roll forward like the tide, and white people will drown in their own hypocrisy.

When the pastor called for a walking collection, Dan took his place in the line of black worshippers snaking up the aisles and along the Communion rail in full view of everyone present. He reached the huge basket held by the usher at the foot of the pulpit and emptied his pockets. No beer for him this Sunday. And without beer, no NFL. Who needed the NFL anyway? This was a day the Lord hath made, and he would rejoice and be glad in it. He bowed his head as the preacher pronounced the Benediction. He stumbled after the congregation through the wide-open doors and into the sunlight.

"Thank you for being among us," the preacher said, flashing his gold tooth and seizing Dan's hand in a grasp which left no doubt as to who was superior. "Come again, please. All are welcome in God's sight." Dan backed away, bowing slightly, smiling, feeling better than he had in years. He moved swiftly up the sidewalk toward home, in the buzz all around him, his body humming.

Bill Eldridge gently swirled the remaining gin in his glass before holding it up to reflect the magenta glow of the setting sun. He stretched out his legs so his topsiders rested easily on the porch railing. "Good sail," he said.

"Yes, a good sail," agreed Dan, taking possession of Bill's glass. "Aren't we blessed. What more can a man want than a fresh breeze, a stiff drink, and a comfortable rocking chair?" He stood up. "I'll order you another short one, on my tab."

As he waited his turn at the bar he glanced at the weather report on the small color tv screen mounted above the popcorn machine. He heard a voice behind him. Over his shoulder, he saw Clark Doubeck squinting at the screen. "Good goddamn!" said Clark.

"Weatherman's a nerd," said Dan. "Calls himself a meteorologist. Why don't they hire weather reporters who look like they've been out in the weather? Retired tugboat captain could do the job. Better still, a fisherman. Somebody with salt on his lips and windburn on his cheeks."

"That's not what I'm looking at," said Clark. "You see that tropical disturbance west of Cape Verde Islands? Doesn't look good."

Dan flashed a right angle at the bartender with his thumb and index finger and watched the crystal-clear gin spill over ice in two glasses. Bill Eldridge would be on his ass by the time Jerianne made her appearance. Serve her right. If she didn't stop coming up pregnant, Bill would have to sell his Jay-30 to feed all the mouths at their table. Then what would give meaning to his life? He'd be just another Allstate adjuster bored with his job.

"What's this, the fourth, maybe fifth disturbance we've seen this season? Nothing to worry about." Dan lifted a glass in each hand and headed toward the porch. "Though come to think of it, the blues are kind of out of whack."

Making his way through the throng of Club members to the spot Bill Eldridge staked out as his own, Dan saw the bronze back and shoulders of a woman in a black halter dress, hair tied in a ponytail with a leather strip, and on her feet, which rested on the rung of the adjacent rocking chair, leather sandals with narrow straps criss-crossing shapely ankles, but not obscuring her silver anklet. Her toenails were painted magenta, a bold color not usually worn by

41

FYC ladies. The man next to her was long and gangly, his hair also in a ponytail tied with a leather strip. Definitely not a Club member. His eye on the woman, Dan eased onto the bench which ran along the porch railing, with his back to the rolling ocean. He handed one gin glass to Bill, who took it eagerly.

"Well, hello," said the woman in the halter dress, shifting in her chair and extending her hand. Silver bracelets jangled on her tan forearm. "Remember me? Windham Doubeck."

"Sorry, I didn't recognize you fully dressed," joked Dan.

"Turn around, Peter," the woman said to the gangly man. "This is Dan McInnes, who saved our catamaran."

"Peter Arnold," said the man. "Thank you for rescuing my wife." His unusual accent almost marked him as a Brit, but not quite. "Windham told me you kept her from being eaten alive by sharks the other day."

Damn disappointing Windham was married, but no surprise. A woman like that wouldn't last long single. "Bluefish," said Dan. "Mean little bastards. We don't get shark attacks in these waters."

"Certainly get them where I come from. Several deaths a year, actually. Though we don't mourn the loss of the foolish tourists who venture into dangerous waters."

"Peter's an Aussie. Grew up in Newcastle. Near Sydney." Windham glanced at Bill Aldridge. "Australia."

Dan should have recognized the accent. He was a fan of Crocodile Dundee. "This is Bill Aldridge," said Dan. "A master sailor in our races." Bill nodded as he inspected his own shoes.

"Peter's a botanist," said Windham. "Studies exotic species. Just back from Peru. On his way to headwaters of the Amazon. Rain forest. Consults for Scripps, National Geographic. That sort of thing."

That sort of thing. Scripps, National Geographic, Australia, Peru. Dan suddenly felt provincial. He had spent his life in Fearrington, with one tour of European cathedrals at Nora's behest. "Your husband is Peter Arnold," he said lamely, "but you're Doubeck."

Windham's laughter jingled in the salt air, like wind chimes made of sea urchin spines. She gazed provocatively into Dan's eyes. "So?"

"Oh, I get it," said Dan. "You're women's lib. Contemporary. Kept your own name when you married." The corners of Windham's eyes crinkled as she smiled. "You expect us Neanderthals in the Southland to know you're husband and wife because you both wear ponytails," Dan zinged her.

Her eyes narrowed. She reached out to touch the signal flag logo embroidered on the pocket of Dan's shirt which Nora had given him for his birthday. "Certainly," she retorted. "Rather like I should be able to tell you and your wife are a matched set because you give off the same signals. She wears hers around her waist, and you wear yours on your chest."

Dan felt his blood pressure rise. He was annoyed by Windham's slick repartee and embarrassed about his shirt. Ordinarily he had the fastest verbal draw, and the last thing he wanted was to be identified with Nora's cutesy couture. "This is a Club Commodore's shirt," he explained. "All the past Commodores wear them, especially on race days." Windham stood up, saluted, reached for his gin glass, took a sip, and lightly spritzed him as she had done at the water spigot.

"I say, Windham, you're a bit feisty this evening," said Peter. "That's no way to show gratitude to the bloke who risked his life to keep your lovely gams attached to your body."

Peter bent over and touched the healing scar on Windham's ankle. "Nasty little wound," he said. "Bloody amazing how deep the puncture went. In Australia we put sea kelp on bites like this."

"Here we mostly deal with jellyfish stings," said Dan. "Best thing is to piss on the sting. Ammonia neutralizes...."

"Daniel! What a thing to say in mixed company!" Nora appeared and sat beside Dan on the bench. "We meet again," she said to Windham. "I apologize for my husband. He sometimes forgets his manners."

"My wife Nora," Dan said to Peter. "Nora, this is Windham's husband Peter Arnold."

Nora arched her eyebrows, staring first at Peter, then at Windham. "I thought your name is Doubeck," she said. "Is your husband Peter-Arnold Doubeck, a double first name? We have double names around here, you know, Mary Margaret or Emmy Lou, but not so much with our men, though a Billy-Bob isn't unheard of." She turned toward Bill

Eldridge. "Does Jerianne—now there's a double name—ever call you Billy-Bob? Billy-Bob and Jerianne." Bill studied his shoes as Nora giggled, and Dan realized she had spent some time at the bar.

"That's how they do it nowadays, Nora, separate last names for husband and wife." He thought he had detected easing of his wife's facial expression when she discovered Windham was married. He watched her eyes dart from ponytail to ponytail. "Peter's a botanist. Exotic species."

"And what exotic species brings you to our environs?" Nora stared at Windham.

"Dionaea muscipula," said Peter.

"Sounds exotic to me," said Nora.

"Named for the Greek goddess of love," Peter said. "White flowers, rosettes of leaves with hinged blades. Insectivore. Perennial. Only grows in this small, finite region of the world."

"Venus flytrap!" Nora was proud of herself for recognizing the description of the plant. She became animated. "When I was a child, we dug them out of the swamp and fed them yellow-headed flies."

"Yes, yes," said Peter. "Common to you natives, exotic to newcomers like me."

Clark Doubeck appeared. "I see you've met my niece Windham and her husband Peter," he said, kneeling on the bench to scan the southeastern horizon. "Week or two, we could be in for a big blow."

"A cyclone!" said Peter. "Hope it's a rip-snorter. I've never experienced one in this part of the world."

"They call them hurricanes here, Darling," said Windham. "I was in one when I was a very small child visiting Uncle Clark. Hazel was her name."

"You were in Hazel?" Clark looked at Windham in astonishment. "Not possible. I don't think of you as old enough..."

Windham laughed. "Oh, but I am, Uncle Clark. I'm not quite the young innocent you remember."

Dan glanced at Windham's youthful appearance and did the math. Hazel was 1954, and it was now 2006, fifty-two years, plus how old Windham was at the time. Clark was correct. Not possible.

47

"You brought me over to this Club during that storm to secure your boat," said Windham. "The wind was so strong it almost blew me off the pier into the sound. By the time you carried me back to the car, the water in the street was up to your knees."

Dan felt both disappointed and relieved by the revelation that Windham was only a decade younger than he was. I suffer from age-bias, he realized, no woman past fifty can be considered sexy. Windham knocked sexy out of the park, and being closer to his age made Dan feel less like a dirty old man. "Hazel was the worst storm ever hit this beach," said Dan. "Tore off the entire roof of the Club, destroyed ladies' and men's dressing rooms. Took the boat docks only God knew where. Don't want another like Hazel."

"Ought keep a weather eye on this new tropical depression," said Clark.

"Oh, look!" Nora pointed toward the beach where the last rays of sun made long shadows. "What's that buggy doing on the strand? Nobody's supposed to drive vehicles out there except lifeguards."

As the buggy drew closer, the man at the wheel blew the horn and waved his hand. He wore a yellow bandanna

48

around his forehead. "That's Jackie Jerrold," said Bill. "Common as dirt. Tattoos on his chest. Rumor is he grows pot inside his cottage. He gets away with most anything. Probably pays off the beach police."

Nora asked, "Where does he come from?"

"Nobody knows," said Bill. "Showed up here couple of years ago, has his finger into everything. Friend of Art Bentley who runs the hotel. Hangs out with that bunch doing construction over at the waterway. Rides a motorcycle sometimes." He warmed to his subject. "Nice house up near the fishing pier, used to be the Caldwell cottage, he renovated it. Some say he put a hot-tub on the upper deck. Not sure where he gets his money. He lives the life of Riley, that's for damn sure."

"Things are changing around here," said Dan. "Used to be you knew everybody at the beach, except for the Marines from up the base. Those were the days. Now we've got all these people from New Jersey moving here in droves, escaping cold winters and high taxes."

"Their money's good," said Bill. "Retirement money. Golden parachutes. Clean."

"Their cars aren't clean," said Dan. "Traffic pollution's so bad I'm thinking of motoring to the Club in my boat, so I won't get tied up in the jam at the drawbridge."

"Lot of daytrippers now," said Bill. "Don't pay for cottages or hotel rooms. Leave their trash on the beach for us to pick up."

Eavesdropping from nearby, Ted Lassiter chimed in. "You know what I heard? Somebody told me they saw a nigger having lunch over here at the Club. Can you imagine that?"

"Can't be true," said Nora. "Not one member would invite a black person to be a guest. And blacks can't get membership, so somebody was pulling your leg."

Dan corrected his wife. "Oh yes, they can become members. Not one word in the rulebook keeping them out."

Nora tapped her fingers on the porch railing. "Of course it's not in the rulebook. I know that. It's a tradition, an understanding we've always had. No blacks, no Jews. And precious few Catholics or Baptists. Episcopalians, Presbyterians, mostly. Several Methodists."

"No Jews?" said Peter. "That seems rather extreme."

"Jews have their own place farther down the beach," said Ted. "Nice club. Not as big as ours, of course, and not a sailing club. More a dining club, with showers and dressing rooms."

"In this day and age," said Peter, "I'm surprised the Club still has these artificial barriers to membership."

"What do you mean artificial?" asked Ted.

"Race and religion," said Windham.

"It's not about race and religion," said Ted. "It's about what you have in common with people you want in your social circle."

"No, it's not," said Windham.

"Of course it is," said Ted. "It's about who loves sailing."

"Is owning a sailboat a requirement for membership?" asked Windham.

"Not exactly. But appreciation for sailing, that's implied in the Club's name."

"So all the sailboats are yachts?" Clark interrupted his sky watch. "Don't pay my niece too much mind. She's always liked to put a little vinegar in your greens."

"Why can't a Jew who loves sailing be welcome to membership?" asked Windham. "Or an African-American who owns a yacht?"

"Good god, Peter, put a muzzle on your wife," said Ted. "She's a loose cannon."

"She has a good point," said Dan, once more coming to Windham's rescue.

"What is her point?" asked Ted.

"My point is," said Windham, "the color of someone's skin or their house of worship has nothing whatsoever to do with the recreation of sailing."

"Never been a colored sailor in the America's Cup," said Ted. "Coloreds don't take to water."

"If you don't want Jews or blacks, state it in Club membership rules," said Windham.

"Look here, Missy, you're going too far," said Clark. "Lighten up. You don't understand how things are. If we put it in Club rules, we'd open ourselves to discrimination lawsuits."

"If you don't like the way we run things, why are you here partaking of our Southern hospitality? Maybe you don't fit in," said Ted.

"She fits in just fine," said Dan.

"Sounds like a carpetbagger to me." Ted jabbed his forefinger at Windham. "You and your kind try to upset the natural order of things. White should stay with white, colored with colored, Christians with Christians, Jews with Jews."

"Now you get off my niece's back," said Clark. "She grew up in California, which is a whole different part of the USofA."

"Windham works with all kinds of people," said Peter. "She's dedicated to equal opportunity."

"Where does she work?," asked Ted. "For the ACLU?"

Peter started to reply, but Windham put her hand on his arm. "I work for a nonprofit called Grassroots, connected with Berkeley School of Journalism."

"Some kind of landscaping business?" asked Bill with a smirk. "Lotta illegals in that line of work."

"I work with migrants up at Mount Gilead," said Windham. "Sort of a journalist. Document that way of life."

"I knew it!" said Ted. "Outside agitator. Can't you leave well enough alone? Go back to California, where you've all those pregnant Mexican illegals coming over the border to have us American citizens pay for the births of their bastard children. We don't want that kind of thing in North Carolina. Got enough problem with lazy coloreds on the welfare. "

Windham turned away. "Uncle Clark, would you fetch me a nice tall cool one? Peter and I will toast the sunset and call it a day."

"I wonder," mused Peter, "since the Club keeps out blacks and Jews, how about homosexuals? Are they tolerated, or do you rip their Club logos off their shirts?"

Clark stood up. "You like a garnish with this round?" he asked Windham.

"Not necessary," she said.

"I have noticed," continued Peter, "that I am the only man present whose hair reaches below his earlobes. Is this a Club rule? Perhaps I should visit the Club barber, lest anyone assume I am not, what is it you say, a good old boy."

Bill and Ted stared out to sea, pretending not to hear Peter's comment. At that moment, Dan took a liking to Peter Arnold, and also envied him his freedom to say and do as he wished without regard to social convention, roaming the four corners of the world with feisty Windham waiting for him dockside.

.

Yellows

When the yellow warning flag is flown,

ocean conditions are subject to rapid

change, and swimmers should proceed

with caution.

Rule 22

Fearrington Yacht Club Handbook

Dan recognized Windham's voice on the phone. "I'm hopping mad," she said. "Peter says forget it, to hell with these fools, but he's a peacenik and I'm not. I don't want to presume upon our new friendship, but you've been a Commodore and a judge, and I hope you can advise me of my rights."

"Calm down," said Dan. "What's happened?"

"This registered letter from the Fearrington Yacht Club makes my blood boil."

"Let me take a chair. Okay, read it to me."

Windham cleared her throat. "'Dear Mrs. Doubeck. Right there, at the start, Mrs.. There is no Mrs. Doubeck. Clark Doubeck is my uncle, not my spouse. I am married to Peter Arnold, and there is no Mrs. Arnold. I am Ms. Windham Doubeck."

"That it? That's all? Maybe the Club manager called you Mrs. because Clark told him you're married. Wives get listed in the computer with Mrs. before their last names."

"Are husbands listed as Mr.?"

"Of course not. They're listed last name, first name. Unmarried members are listed same way, last name, first name. You're making a mountain out of a...."

Windham persisted. "How would you like to be Mr...what was your wife's maiden name?"

"Nelson."

"She'd be Nora Nelson and you'd be Mr. Nelson."

"Don't be silly."

"Well, I would feel silly as Mrs. Arnold, which is why I kept my own name."

"Is this what's got you so riled up? How can I advise you of your rights? Your rights to what?"

"It's what they say in the body of the letter."

"Read me the offensive part, or I'll start charging you my hourly consultation fee."

Again she cleared her throat. "It has been brought to our attention that Club members witnessed you swimming in the ocean wearing inappropriate attire, to wit, wet, clinging blue jeans and a transparent white t-shirt, rather than a ladies' bathing suit. You then were witnessed traversing private Club property, to wit, the Club porch, in self-same outfit." Windham's voice grew louder. "And here's the most offensive part: A woman your age should know better than to appear In public in such a revealing garment. We hereby request that you apologize in writing to the Board, promising never again to engage in such unbecoming conduct, or we shall have to suspend your guest privileges indefinitely, and blacklist you for membership.

"Then comes the coup de grace: You owe your uncle Clark Doubeck, a former Commodore with a stellar reputation, respect and gratitude for recommending you for Club status."

"Whoa!" said Dan. "You making up this letter as a joke?"

"Just delivered. I had to sign for it."

"They described you as a woman of your age. How old is a woman of your age?"

"I don't see how that's relevant."

"If you're to be my client, you answer my questions. Understood?"

"Yessir, Commodore sir! I'm fifty-six years old."

"A mere slip of a girl."

"Don't make fun of me. How old are you?"

"Touche'," said Dan. "Sixty-eight. Old codger."

"You don't seem old to me."

"I don't date my clients. Especially when they're married."

"Stop flirting with me. This is serious. They're threatening to take away my guest privileges, and Uncle Clark is putting me up for membership."

"Did you swim in a white t-shirt?"

"Yes, I did. And cut-off jeans."

"Which day of the week?"

"Sunday."

Sunday, while Dan was participating in the Free Will Baptist Church service. He tut-tutted her. "The Lord's Day? Heaven forbid. Must've been after church. Club members don't show up until Sunday afternoons, when they've made the obligatory church appearance and taken Big Mama out for seafood lunch."

"I planned to go diving with Peter, on the wrecks off shore. He says that's where the fish swarm."

"Indeed they do."

"We had trouble with Uncle Clark's boat, and it was a hot day, so I jumped into the water in my shorts and shirt, left my swimsuit aboard with my scuba gear. When the boat wouldn't start, I came into the Club to shower off in the ladies' dressing room."

"I take it you're certified?"

"Of course. In Australia, we dive off the Great Barrier Reef."

"I'm certified, too," said Dan. "Dive off Fort Fisher for Civil War artifacts."

"Peter likes to photograph exotic plant life. Says the continental shelf off Cape Fear, with the Gulf Stream, creates interesting species. But I prefer to look at the brilliant colors under water."

"Back to the subject at hand," said Dan. "You crossed the Club porch to get to the ladies' dressing room?"

"Of course. But I didn't cross the white line."

"See any older ladies on the porch in rocking chairs?"

"A few."

"One of 'em have hair a startling blue color?"

"Yes! She stared at me."

"That's who made the complaint," said Dan. "Margaret Monmouth, with her widow contingent. She's the Club's grand dame, appointed herself supervisor of protocol, especially when it involves attractive young women. She reigns, and no one dares challenge her domain. If Mrs. Monmouth speaks, the Board members listen. I recommend you placate the Board by sending a letter of apology. I can word it for you. That should take care of the matter. The Board will inform Mrs. Monmouth you have bowed to her power, and nothing more will be made of it."

"I've no intention of apologizing," said Windham, "not in this lifetime."

"Then they'll suspend you. For awhile. Maybe even a whole day, so they can tell Mrs. Monmouth they acted on her complaint. Slap you on the wrist."

"Screw the Board."

"How far you want to go with this?"

"I want them to apologize to me."

Dan stifled a sigh. "Would you like a public apology?"

"That would work for me."

"I've been itching to try a case," said Dan, "after so many years on the bench. This could be my last hurrah." He heard an intake of breath. "Calm down. I was making a joke. You're not a felon. You've only committed an affront to Club policy. The annual meeting is scheduled for Wednesday. If you'll provide me the letter, I'll handle this for you."

"I'll make it up to you," said Windham. "for saving my Hobie and saving my Club access."

"Don't tempt me with your wiles. And don't feel obligated to attend the meeting. Right now you're a seasonal guest member, not a voting member. I can handle this without you being present."

"I'll take that under consideration," said Windham. "I'll bring the letter within the hour."

The Board members sat in their usual pecking order at the long table in the ballroom, exchanging greetings. A scanty representation of Club membership faced the Board in rows of folding chairs. Spotting Margaret Monmouth in the third row, Dan warmed to his task. Time for him to retrieve those whereases and heretofores from wherever he banished them when he retired as a jurist. He must liberally sprinkle them over these jackasses until they hollered 'nuff.

Commodore Watson called the meeting to order and worked down the agenda of Old Business. Water spigots and rusty nails. Bar hours and parking stickers. Swing set for the children's playground. New boat hoist. Place mats with the Club logo for the weekly ladies' bridge luncheons. Dan was glad he was a past Commodore. He'd lost his appetite for sitting through this stuff. Then the Board took up New Business, and the ballroom suddenly was packed with members. Windham slipped into the seat next to him, and he saw Mrs. Monmouth glare at her. No doubt who was responsible for the complaint against Windham.

Dan rose and addressed the Board. "We've a matter to attend to which is of utmost importance, since an effort has been made to besmirch the reputation of a fine lady among us."

The Commodore glanced quickly at Windham as a murmur went around the room. "I don't think that's necessary this evening, Judge," he said. "The Board is handling the matter in closed session."

Dan walked to the front of the room, holding high the letter of complaint. "Miz Doubeck—and I do stress the Miz, since there is no Miz-iz Doubeck, our highly-esteemed past Commodore Clark Doubeck never having been to the altar—Miz Doubeck, whom you see before you in the fourth row next to my empty chair, wishes the notice of complaint to be read aloud so the full membership can be apprised of the anonymous charge made against her by an as-yet-unidentified Club member, which initiated the action you have heretofore threatened."

"I don't think this is the time or place," stammered the Commodore.

"Ms. Doubeck is entitled to receive a full accounting for her alleged transgression, and to face her accuser, if she is to adequately defend herself. That is the American way." Dan stared at Margaret Monmouth, her face rigid below her blue hair.

"I don't have at my disposal the letter in question," said the Commodore. "Perhaps after this evening's meeting we can discuss this in the Club office." The other Board members nodded assent. Dan read aloud the letter to Wiindham and placed it on the table in front of the Commodore. "Now I shall commence Ms. Doubeck's defense," he said, "as I introduce into evidence visual aids relevant to the issue at hand." A murmur again went around the room, and all eyes were fixed on Dan as he pulled down the projection screen behind the conference table and plugged in the slide projector he had set up prior to the meeting. "Will someone please douse the lights," he said. "You gentlemen of the Board might wish to swivel in your chairs so you may view the screen."

"This isn't necessary, Judge," pleaded the Commodore.

Dan aligned the bright rectangle on the screen and clicked the first slide into view. "We have the lovely Ms. Windham Doubeck in this photograph," he said. "See there, her ponytail, that should give you sufficient reference." The Board mumbled assent.

"You see she is wearing cut-off levis which reach her kneecaps. And a white t-shirt upon which is imprinted PickledPepperPickersPreferProperComPensation."

"Cute," someone whispered.

"Yes, yes," said the Commodore, "please get to your point."

"If you observe closely," said Dan, "as an anonymous Club member has already observed closely, you can see Ms. Doubeck is sopping wet." The Board and the membership leaned forward to scrutinize the screen.

"Yes, yes," said the Commodore. "This is what was reported to us, that the person in question had walked onto the Club porch in just such attire. But where did you get the photograph?"

"I hosed her down," said Dan. "Simple as that." A titter went around the room as Dan walked up to the screen, the light from the projector making him one with the image of Windham. Dan brought his face close to the image and scrutinized it up and down. "I fail to see what is objectionable about Ms. Doubeck's attire."

"Stop being facetious, Judge," said the Commodore. "You know darn well what we mean."

Dan stepped away from the screen. "No, no, I don't," he said, "and neither does Ms. Doubeck. Is there a Club bias against pickled peppers? We've a-plenty of them in the Club refrigerator, especially piccalilli relish." Several Club members laughed out loud.

"Commodore Watson," said Dan, "please step up to the screen and point out what inspired you to send Ms. Doubeck a notice of complaint."

The Commodore waved his arm in the light from the projector, making shadows across the screen. "There, there," he said with considerable irritation.

"Where, where?" asked Dan. "Which part of her clothing violates Club decorum? Is it the sleeves of her shirt, which reach her elbows?"

♦

"No, no, of course not."

"Do you find her jeans too short, too long, too tight?"

"Dammit, Judge, you're taking this too far," said the Commodore.

Dan again leaned close in to the screen. He touched his finger to the right and left of the PepperPickers slogan. "Could it be that a Club member imagined that she saw—and I use the female pronoun to refer to this anonymous complainant because I cannot imagine a male member—please excuse the pun—making such an objection to the lovely sight of Ms. Doubeck--could it be that this complainant believed she saw—brace yourselves, gentlemen and gentle ladies, for I must of necessity use the common terms for the female anatomy—believed she saw nipples, better known as tits, and sometimes referred to by the less refined as boobies or hooters—forgive me, Mrs. Monmouth, for I do not mean to offend your sensibilities—believed she saw these anatomical objects, bestowed by Nature for suckling infants, beneath Ms. Doubeck's sea-soaked shirt?" Guffaws went up from male Club members.

Dan indicated the lower portion of the image on the screen. "Surely nothing was visible through the thick blue denim of the pants. So by process of elimination, it must

71

have been something in the vicinity of the shirt which provoked the complaint. I invite anyone present to come forward and demonstrate, using this image on the screen, precisely the nature of the offending body part, and describe in your own words what you find offensive. Do I have any takers?"

No one responded. Dan continued, "Commodore Watson, looking at this color photograph, would you characterize Ms. Doubeck's nipples as being pink, brown, or some other distinctive shade, and please describe how light or dark female nipples may be—I specify female nipples because at the beach we all are treated to the sight of male nipples on a daily basis, some more or less prominent depending on the age of the owner—pray tell us, how dark may female nipples be, beneath the fabric of a shirt, before they violate the Club standard of appropriateness?"

Dan clicked the next image onto the screen. "In the absence of a reply, I shall proceed." A photograph from the *Fearrington Citizen* appeared, with the caption *Commodore's Wife Capsizes in Ladies' Boat Race*. Nora McInnes was clearly recognizable holding onto the mast of a Sunfish as she was towed to shore. Her hair was dishevelled, her Club polo shirt plastered against her torso by the dunking she had just received at the behest of a maverick breeze.

"I shall declare this meeting adjourned," said the Commodore.

"No, no!" came a response from those assembled.

"Here you see a female Club member," said Dan, "to wit, the wife of a Commodore, soaking wet from her encounter with a fickle sea. I present this with all due respect, as a precedent in the matter at hand. And I recall no complaint made against Mrs. McInnes for communing with the sea in inappropriate attire. Whereas Ms. Doubeck was singled out for similar appearance."

He clicked Nora's image off the screen. "I have one last piece of evidence," he said, "which will demonstrate the lack of equity extant in this notice of complaint." He clicked on an image of Board members disembarking from the Committee Boat on a race day. Areas of the image were circled with a marker. Buddy Watson's polo shirt was separated from his pants, his ample naked belly in plain view. Ted Lassiter's right leg reached for the dock, his left leg maintaining his balance on the boat, so that his swim trunks exposed a portion of his gonads.

A gasp went around the room, and Dan immediately clicked off the projector. "Lights, please." The membership sat blinking. Mrs. Monmouth made haste to leave the room. "What I have just shown you suggests there may be a personal motive in the persecution of Ms. Doubeck," Dan said. "The Fearrington Yacht Club has always functioned with a well-established rule of etiquette which allows us to enjoy our shared space. Polite behavior dictates that we avert our eyes and pretend not to notice potentially embarrassing exposure. We do not call attention to such events. This is a sportsman's club, and the complaint against Ms. Doubeck is not in keeping with good sportsmanship. The Board, and a certain Club member who now seems to have stepped out of the room, owe Windham Doubeck a profound apology which, I feel certain, she will gracefully accept."

"This matter has been taken to the ultimate absurdity," said the Commodore. "But I move we rescind our notice of complaint and remove it from our Club membership files. Do I hear a second to my motion?"

"Second," said Ted Lassiter.

"All in favor say aye and I shall declare this meeting adjourned," said the Commodore.

74

"Most fun I've ever had at an annual meeting," said someone to Dan on the way out the door.

Clark Doubeck clapped him on the back. "Fine job, Judge," he said. "My niece got herself a good lawyer." He leaned close to Dan's ear. "You knew all along it was Margaret Monmouth, didn't you? Let's hope this shuts her up once and for all."

Younger Club members stopped to congratulate Dan and express their apologies to Windham for what she had been put through. "Thank god Nora stayed home," said Jerianne. "She would have been mortified to see herself up on the screen."

"Actually," Dan said, "she's the one who gave me the news clipping for Windham's defense. Nora may be peculiar, but she's on the side of justice, truth, and the American Way."

"That was a selfless thing for your wife to do," said Windham. "I'll have to thank her for caring about me."

"She doesn't care about you," said Dan. "She doesn't like you one bit. But she cares about doing the right thing, and you were being done wrong."

Windham gave Dan a hug. "I thank you from the bottom of my heart for standing in my defense even though you thought I was being silly."

Dan put his arm around Windham's shoulders and escorted her onto the porch. "No need to thank me. Purely selfish. If they suspend you, who would light up my life down here? I'm becoming quite fond of you, you know."

"I know," said Windham. "Likewise."

"**W**hy *Mandamus*?" asked Windham.

"As in writ of," said Dan. "Means absolute duty. To go sailing." He took her hand. "Watch your step. Teak can be slippery when wet."

Windham steadied herself in the cockpit. "Gorgeous boat. Why must you feel it's your duty to go sailing? Seems like you'd want to just for fun."

"Protestant ethic."

"If you invited me here out of a sense of duty, I'm leaving right now."

"I invited you because you're beautiful and full of spirit, and my boat's beautiful, and the weather's beautiful, and I have a duty to honor all things bright and beautiful. Now will you go for a sail with me?"

"Doesn't Nora want to sail? With all the signal flags she wears, I would think she's an old salt."

"Not for a long time," said Dan. "Not since....uh oh, wind's striking up. Better make haste while the sun shines." He switched on the engine, cast off the mooring lines, and maneuvered out of his slip.

"Glorious!" said Windham as they motored down the channel toward the inlet. She scanned the shore. "Look at all those gigantic new homes! Where do people get their money?"

"Beats me. I'm just a country boy."

"Where are you talking me in your water chariot?"

"It's a Hinckley. Best boatmaker, in my opinion. I've had my sloop a long time. Secret's in keeping it maintained."

"You never said where we're going."

"Said the owl to the pussycat, to the land where the bong tree grows," answered Dan.

"Bong tree? I thought marijuana was an illegal crop in North Carolina."

"We're sailing to ten-mile reef. And I don't mean reefer." Windham made a face at him. "Gulf Stream's not far offshore," he said. "On a day like today, with a light wind, water's pure magic."

He guided *Mandamus* past the channel markers and put on speed in the choppy inlet, where several fishing boats lined up with the rock jetty. He pointed toward a large ship near the horizon. "Oil tanker. Hate those things. Damn companies jockeying to install rigs and pump oil off our coast. If they make a spill, you can kiss fishing goodbye." On the ocean side of the inlet, he cut the engine and hoisted the sails, which soon luffed. The boom swung lazily. "Wind died." He started the engine and lowered the sails. Windham leaned back on the deck, October sun warm on her face and legs. She listened to the purr of the engine and the sound of the sea slipping past the hull. The next thing she knew, Dan was calling her out of her trance. "We're here!" He threw out the Danforth anchor. "Put on your swimsuit and we'll go for a dive." He lifted the lid to the storage unit on the port side and brought forth two face masks and two air tanks.

"A dive? I thought you were just taking me for a sail," said Windham as she sat up. "You didn't warn me you had a hidden agenda." She stood up, pulled off her shirt and stepped out of her shorts. "I'm wearing my swimsuit. I travel light."

Dan gave her an approving glance. "I like that. Nora travels like the Duchess of Windsor. Her entire world goes with her."

"Let's not diss our spouses," said Windham. "Let's enjoy what we have to offer each other without dragging them into it." She scanned the western horizon. "What happened to the beach? I see nothing but sea and sky."

"That's why I love it out here. Nobody knows where I am, and nobody can reach me if I turn off my ship-to-shore. Which I just did." He pulled off his shirt, put on his tank and mask and jumped overboard, holding his fins.

Windham donned her gear and leapt in after him, bobbed to the surface and swam long strokes to join him. Together they dived fifteen feet, and together rose to the surface amid silvery bubbles of exhale. "Let's do it again!" she shouted, diving deeper.

When they surfaced, he blew out his mouthpiece and tapped his wrist. "Let's dive to the wreck. Only forty feet down. We've thirty minutes of air."

Dan led the way down to the wreck, where the rusting hull of a Liberty ship appeared in diffused light. Silvery sheepshead swam dreamily through the green gel. Dan pointed upward toward a giant skate cruising overhead. Then he realized Windham was farther and farther away, mesmerized by the shapes and colors, losing her sense of time and place in these unfamiliar waters. A rainbow of fish swarmed her. He swam in her direction, touched her arm, and pointed to his watch. They began their ascent, trailing bubbles. When they broke the surface in the midday sun, he chided her. "Watch out for rapture of the deep."

Back aboard *Mandamus*, Dan laid a small object on the hatch and chipped at it gently with a ballpeen hammer until scale broke free and exposed a smooth metallic surface with a tiny opening on one end. "Hardware from a German sub," he said. "Thoroughly scavenged a long time ago.

When I get lucky I find a remnant." He placed the artifact in her palm.

"German sub?" asked Windham. "This close to Carolina Beach?"

"During the war, Nazi subs were up and down our coast. Legend goes that a couple of Nazi seamen snuck into the beach theatre one night, to see, ironically, *Watch on the Rhine*. Yacht Club was in blackout after dark during that period, boat races on hold. My father rode horse patrol, kept lookout for the enemy."

"The enemy." said Windham, "When we dispose of one, we find another. England, Spain, Germany, Japan, Vietnam, Russia, Iran, Iraq, Cuba. When we're short of foreigners, we make war on domestic enemies, blacks, homosexuals, and now Latinos. Even in teeny-tiny provincial Mount Gilead up the road."

"Nature of mankind," said Dan.

"Might interest you to know there are some societies which are not adversarial," said Windham. "But that's a subject for a rainy day. I want to do some free-diving."

Dan reached out and wiped her upper lip with his forefinger. "Nosebleed," he said. "Little bit of a trickle. Wait until it stops before we go back in the water. Don't want you to be shark bait."

Windham pressed her knuckles against her nostrils and let her head roll back. "Always happens when I deep-dive. Maybe that's why I'm not adversarial. I'm a bleeder."

"I know," said Dan. "That's how we met." He pointed toward her foot. "But you sure are adversarial when you want to be. Put the Yacht Club Board in its place."

To his welcome surprise, Windham removed her swimsuit and soon they were both skinny-dipping in the green sea, salt water cool against their bodies. Windham frog-kicked underwater, surfaced, and turned onto her back, eyes closed against the bright sun.

Dan swam beside her. "Love your nipples," he said. "Like a mermaid. Margaret Monmouth would go ballistic if she saw you defiling her ocean."

Windham rolled onto her belly and spread her arms wide so she could float effortlessly, hair swirling about her face. Dan touched her buttocks. "Love your ass," he said. "Way it catches the sun." Windham swam to the boat, kicking water in Dan's face as he followed her. "I'm a gentleman," he said when they reached the ladder. "Ladies first."

Windham mooned him as she ascended. She turned and bent over the stern, allowing her breasts to swing free. Dan made a grab for the ladder, but she jerked it out of reach. "Promise you'll keep your hands off me, you lecher, or you can swim with the sharks."

"I promise," he said, and she let the ladder back down. The moment he set his feet on deck, he wrapped his arms around her.

Windham protested, "You said you'd keep your hands off me."

"I lied. You know why sharks won't attack lawyers?"

"Nope." Pushing him away, Windham pulled on her shirt and shorts.

"Professional courtesy."

"No more lawyer jokes, please." She handed Dan his swim trunks. "Put your pants on, Counselor, since I can't trust you." She rummaged in the ice chest and extracted two bottles of Yuengling, asking, "How'd you know this is my favorite beer?" Popping off the top, she took a swig. "Why is it beer seems colder than any other beverage?" She hiccupped. "And why does it cause me to hiccup?"

Dan popped the top off his bottle. "The Bench responds to your queries: my favorite, too…something about hops and malt… and hell, I don't know, maybe your epiglottis is out of whack."

"Takes a strong man to admit he doesn't know something, especially when he can pronounce epiglottis." said Windham. "I have one more question to which I hope you know the answer. What's the bedroom status of your marriage with Nora? You seemed a bit over-eager to take hold of me."

"Don't be coy," said Dan. "Surely you realize a naked woman provokes a naked man, even at my advanced age?"

"Just so you weren't expecting quid pro quo in payment for your legal services at the annual Club meeting."

"You asked about Nora. It's the usual long-term marriage in its sunset years."

"I have no frame of reference for this."

"The missus and I don't make the beast with two heads any more, to use an unromantic euphemism. We've more of a companionate relationship."

"Sorry about that."

"Your turn, quid pro quo. How about your love life?"

"With Peter?"

"Of course with Peter. He's your husband, for god sake." The hum of a boat motor grew louder. Dan looked over his shoulder. "You reckon somebody's spying on us out here?"

"Oh sure," said Windham. "The CIA. They keep tabs on me wherever I am. Labor organizers are a threat to public order."

"You didn't answer my question."

"Peter and I are still in touch. Sometimes. Few and far between. Right before he leaves on a consult, right after he returns. During the interim, not much going on."

"That's difficult to believe." Dan reached out and touched Windham's shoulder. "Beautiful as you are. What is Peter, a pansy?"

Windham laughed. "Certainly not. He's a self-absorbed photographer. Will be away on assignment the next couple of months."

"If I were your husband, I'd never let you out of my sight, much less go on a daylong boat ride with a lawyer."

"Peter doesn't own me. Nor I him. We respect each other's right to conduct our lives as we individually see fit, no questions asked."

"Of course, a modern marriage," said Dan. "Do you have children?"

Windham stood up and turned her back to him, staring at the horizon. "I wanted children, Peter didn't. We married during zero population growth. He felt we had an environmental obligation not to reproduce. So he got clipped." She turned back to Dan. "And you? Children?"

"Long story. Suffice it to say I had a son once. Let's leave it at that for now."

He started up the engine, and they motored to the Club without further conversation. When they disembarked, he set the ice chest down on the dock. "You want another cold one?"

"Skipper, that was a good sail," said Windham. "Even without any wind." She lightly kissed him on the mouth. "I think it's best I depart."

"I was hoping I could provide you a tour of the interior of the cabin," said Dan. "That was my ulterior motive."

"Call me the next time you want to go out."

Dan gave her a thumbs up and watched her walk toward her four-runner. He knew it wouldn't be long before he rang her on the phone.

Dan heard a flushing sound, and Nora came out of the bathroom wiping her mouth with the back of her hand. "I wish you'd stop doing that," he said. "It's not good for you."

She peered into the mirror over her dressing table and applied lipstick. "I wish you'd stop screwing that Doubeck woman." Her voice was low.

He went over to stand next to her. "What did you say?"

"You heard me."

"Now wait a minute. All I did was represent her before the Board, favor to her Uncle Clark. Margaret Monmouth been putting ideas into your head?"

"You were seen aboard *Mandamus*. By an impeccable source."

Dan remembered the boat motoring past as he sat close to Windham in the cockpit. Sonofabitch, the rumor mill was on alert. "You misunderstand," he said. "Do we have to talk about this before we go to the party? Because if we do, we'll probably be late."

"You took her for a sail."

"Indeed I did. I take a lot of people sailing, because my wife no longer goes to sea."

"Must have been a long sail. You didn't return for hours." Nora fluffed her hair.

"Dammit, Nora, if you're going to conduct an inquisition...."

"I'm not. Because I know the truth and I know you'll lie about it. I warn you, there's already talk around the Club." She sprayed her hair and smoothed her eyebrows. "That performance you put on at the annual meeting. And kissing when you brought her in from sailing. People can add two and two."

"All right!" Dan knotted his tie and slipped his wallet into the inside pocket of his navy blue sport coat. "Have it your way. Listen to your gossipy friends."

"I believe Jerianne," said Nora. "She has no guile. Can't do anything but speak the truth."

Dan bit his lip. Damn Jerianne. He'd have to tell Bill to tell his wife to keep her mouth shut and mind her own business.

Nora straightened her back and held her head high. "I am having my own way," she said. "I've a new friend, too."

"What friend? Have I met her?"

"It's a him, and you haven't met, though you've seen him on the beach."

"Who is he?"

"Me to know and you to find out. I'll tell you this much, unlike the Doubeck woman, my new friend isn't married."

Dan was surprised. It wasn't like Nora to play games. "Who the fuck is he?"

"Why, Daniel, you've become a potty-mouth since you met Miz Doubeck." Nora emphasized the Miz. "My friend is Jackie Jerrold."

"That scumbag who rides up and down the beach past the Club? I don't believe you. He's not your type."

Nora looked at Dan triumphantly. "That's what makes him interesting."

Dan headed for the bedroom door. "Now that we've established parameters, let's go to the party and play how-you? fine how you? People will whisper as we pass by, since Jerianne says we're the talk of the town."

"**A**nswer the phone, please," called Nora. "I'm putting on my pantyhose."

Dan set down his Sunday paper. Long ago, the sight of Nora pulling up her stockings would have turned him on. Now it filled him with repugnance. He picked up the ringing phone. "This tropical disturbance has become a tropical depression," said Clark Doubeck. "Now it's got a name. Flossie. What's your opinion?"

"Flossie's a redneck name."

"Stop joshing. Who cares about the name? It's whether she's headed our way," said Clark.

Dan retrieved the back page of the first section. "Nothing much about it in the paper. My opinion is I wouldn't worry."

"Been looking at the weather channel. Tropical depression's strengthened, moving west."

"Get a dozen of those things every year," said Dan. "In the long run, they're full of sound and fury, signifying nothing."

"We're about due for a big blow. Mostly quiet since Charley."

"You worry too much. Fix yourself a bloody mary."

When Dan hung up the phone, he saw Nora standing beside his ugly-chair, which she considered a blemish on her carefully-decorated interior landscape. She was dressed in her church outfit, pinning her hat onto her head. "I don't suppose I could talk you into going to St. Philip's with me," she said. "Might lay to rest some of the gossip."

"Appearing in church together won't put the quietus on the rumor mill. That horse is out of the barn." He paused. "Or I should say, the boat is out of the dock." He settled back into his chair. "Pray for my redemption, Nora. Put an extra twenty bucks into the collection plate on my behalf. And for heaven's sake, stop nagging at me." He felt mean, but one of them had to face things squarely. Their marriage had been in trouble ever since they lost their son.

Nora turned away from him. "Who was that on the phone?" Suspicion tinged her voice.

"Maybe it was your boyfriend Jackie Jerrold."

She turned back around. "He wouldn't call here on a Sunday morning. He knows I go to church."

"While you're praying for salvation, he's probably banging some bimbo in his hot tub."

Nora slapped him hard, so his ears rang. "You win. No more living under the same roof to keep up appearances. I want you out of here."

He rubbed his cheek. "On what grounds?"

"You've ruined everything. People are talking about us."

"They sure must be, the proper Nora McInnes hanging out with that reprobate Jerrold. You two are an oxymoron."

Nora held tightly onto her handbag. "If you hadn't let yourself get seduced by that hussy, I'd never have given Jackie the time of day. I had to pay you back somehow, let you know how it feels."

"Windham is not a hussy. And she's not arrogant. Unlike you and the wives of our friends, she works for a living. With migrants up at Mount Gilead." Dan wanted to tell Nora an affair with Windham had never been consummated, but then he'd have to explain his advances had been rebuffed.

"You're beneath contempt," said Nora. "You never ever wanted me to work. Rather have me keep your home nice, be available to attend Bar functions. At our age, when you're enjoying retirement, you think I'm supposed to carve out a career? Get real."

"I hope you're enjoying eating bonbons with Jackie Jerrold. Because with Jerrold you've nullified any adultery you allege took place with Windham."

Nora's eyes narrowed. "Always the lawyer. Thinking of angles. When we lost Toby, you were busy reading the fine print in the accidental death policy." Her voice caught as Dan winced. "You didn't answer my question. Who was on the phone?"

"Clark Doubeck."

"What did he want?"

"The usual. Weather. You know Clark. Lives alone, nothing else to do but read his barometer and plot storms."

Nora took a book from the shelf and threw it at him. He read the title: *Losing Malcolm.* Cover photo of a baby's hand holding onto an adult thumb. By someone named Henderson. "You should try reading this," said Nora. "That mother knows what it feels like." She slammed the door behind her as she exited.

Women's literature. Dan set the book aside and tried to bring down his blood pressure by turning to the Lifestyle section of the newspaper. He never read it when it was titled Women's Page. As Society Page, he seldom gave it a glance. Now it was Lifestyle, articles by men who cooked meals and took children on play-dates with other children. Sign of the times, cultural change. Last year, a businesswoman and a female attorney had submitted their names for membership in the historic Fearrington Men's

94

Club downtown, causing a rumor they were lesbians. What to do? The FMC would no longer be a haven for Fearrington's prominent males to escape domesticity at all-male banquets, peruse *Playboy* and *Penthouse* magazines, tell dirty jokes. Women would be in their midst. Wives would want to join, keep an eye on husbands who might be consorting with new female members. He had heard women were threatening to sue Augusta National Golf Club, a revered male preserve. The FMC could never survive such a lawsuit, because business was conducted there in the guise of socializing. A lawsuit would open the financial arrangements as well as the membership list, which was not only all-male but all-Caucasian. Next thing you know, the NAACP would be knocking at the magnificently-carved front door, demanding copies of *Ebony* on the parlor tables. He was relieved the Fearrington Yacht Club had wisely elected one female Commodore prior to Watson, as a concession to women's lib. She was the daughter of a former Commodore and had done a fairly good job, careful not to upset the male-dominant apple cart, and had won a couple of sailboat races with her Laser. She earned respect from the Board. But FYC had only members of Caucasian persuasion— hey, he liked that phrase, had a ring to it—he'd have to slip

95

it into his next conversation with Clark, who would roll on the floor laughing.

Now he took notice of the photograph of a beautiful woman in the Lifestyle section. She was wearing a clerical collar, standing in front of a modest white church with St. Ignatius on its marker. St. Ignatius. Where had he heard that before? The article read, "The Reverend Amanda Abingdon has arrived from London to minister to the growing congregation at St. Ignatius. An alternative-lifestyle church, St. Ignatius has quietly blossomed at the corner of Sixth and Queen Streets during the past decade. This reflects a national trend which began in the 1970s at Glide Memorial Church in San Francisco. 'We hope people in every walk of life will join us,' says Reverend Abingdon. Services are Sundays at noon with communion, and gospel singing at seven in the evening.'"

Glide Memorial in San Francisco. Gay church. Fearrington was coming up in the world. Our florists and hairdressers must have reached critical mass, thought Dan, if they're able to support their own house of worship. They sure had become more visible downtown. He could spot them two-by-two at restaurants, and at lest two gay bars were competing for patrons. But why would they need their own church? All these years they had attended

96

well-established churches without incident. Everyone knew Billy Hanford had been gay all his life. He attended St. Philip's with his elderly mother, sat beside her in the Hanford pew in the fourth row below the pulpit, held her hymnal for her. People sometimes gave each other knowing glances, but no one persecuted him. In fact, the congregation appreciated his mellifluous voice when he sang solo at funerals.

There seemed to be some national issue fomenting about homosexual priests in the Episcopal and Catholic churches, though there were gay deacons in the Presbyterian church. Or was it the Methodist? The AIDs thing, that had brought things to a head. Nobody wanted to share a common cup with someone who might be afflicted with HIV, and AIDs sermons were of little interest to mainstream congregations, who heard enough of that subject in television specials. What was that interminably-long play gays had brought to Broadway from England? Something about angels being in America. Gay angels, presumably.

He would have to ask Windham about Glide Church in California. Surely she would be familiar with it, and she might even know of St. Ignatius in Fearrington. Not that she was gay, far from it, but she seemed on the cutting edge of what's happening now.

He felt sorry for parents of gays. Mothers of daughters who would never wear the treasured wedding gown carefully preserved in blue tissue paper, fathers of sons who would never produce grandsons to carry on the family name. How did parents introduce partners of their adult children at family gatherings? I want you to meet my banker son's house companion Bruce? This is my debutante daughter's very very best friend Sheila, wink wink? Had Emily Post or Dear Abby come out with a book of gay etiquette to guide the uninitiated?

Still and all, the lesbian pastor looked like a good enough sort. If he had seen her on the street, he wouldn't have recognized her as gay. Was this the correct term? Seemed like male homosexuals were gay, but female homosexuals were lesbian. Why? Both were about same-sex coupling. Since the term gay had come into popular use meaning homosexual, he had felt it a misnomer. Once it had connoted being happy, joyful, but so many homosexuals were angry, tormented, except perhaps at Fire Island where they partied together without the intrusion of straights. Straight, now there was a word which had taken on new definition. Shortest distance between two points is a straight line. A poker hand of five cards in sequence is a straight. A rehabbed criminal is going straight. Why are heterosexuals now referred to as straight? He knew many heteros who are crooked as the crooked man who walked a crooked mile, a lot of them politicians; why should they be called straight? He would add this to his list titled Questions for God if There is a God, which he would take with him if he stood at the Pearly Gate.

He studied the news photo of Reverend Abingdon. Kind of sexy, waves of dark hair tumbling over her vestment, intelligent eyes, bright smile. Ought to check her out, listen to what she had to say from the pulpit, whether she was more stimulating than Reverend Bradley at St. Philip's. What the hell, he'd done a black church. Why not a gay one? The service was at noon. He had time to make it. Nora would return from St. Philip's ready to continue their hostilities, but she'd find him gone. She'd be furious when he got back and told her he went to church after all, to pray with the Unclean while she paid homage to the patriarchal God of the Church of England.

The modest white frame church sat uneasily at the corner of Sixth and Queen, its narrow front stoop only inches from automobile traffic. Dan took a deep breath before entering. How cliché that St. Ignatius should front on Queen. Was this a deliberate choice of location? Or one of God's politically-incorrect little jokes? Dan hesitated, hoping no one would pass by and recognize him, thinking he'd been hiding in a gay closet all his life. He consoled himself with the thought that since he was now irrevocably branded as a flaming adulterer, though his attempt to make love to Windham was unrequited and he was guilty of nothing more than a momentary lapse of etiquette, his visit to the gay church might be viewed as just another symptom of Judge McInnes' emerging senility. People forgave the elderly for misbehavior, for kicking over the traces, one of the few advantages of aging. You could say outrageous things, make a total fool of yourself, and be regarded as mere entertainment. An old man could pinch the ample bottom of a young woman and not be convicted of sexual assault. An old woman could kick the shin of a police officer and get away with it. Once inside St. Ignatius, he would not be in danger of seeing his friends, who all were straight as an arrow so far as sexual orientation was concerned. Heretofore he had only

100

attended St. Philip's, with that one venture into the black church, whereas....

He mentally slapped himself. Despite his desire to purge himself of legal jargon, he still was doing the heretofores and whereases. He'd have to press hard on his brain's delete button to obliterate forty years of law-school claptrap which obscured the truth of things. Truth was a pariah in the justice system, in that vineyard of bitter fruit where he had long labored. Appearances were its stock in trade. To be rather than to seem was North Carolina's official motto, emblazoned in mosaic at the entrance to the state legislative building. Seeming was the order of the day, rather than being.

How should he present himself at St. Ignatius? As the homophobic good old boy he really was, or as a bleeding-heart liberal who enjoyed hugging people dying of AIDs? Here was his chance to come clean, to be, what was that trendy word? Authentic. What you see is what you get. Straight up. No bullshit. Hi, I'm Dan McInnes, and I'm straight. Well, not exactly straight, not in the narrow sense, because I have fucked around on my wife, back in my younger days before my testosterone level began to decline. But actually, I only did the deed with one woman, and that only for a few months, out of Christian charity, when she needed a shoulder to cry on after her husband took off with someone younger. I was a monogamous philanderer in a committed adulterous relationship with a straight woman, and I did fool Nora without getting caught, and I went straight after that. Am I a fraud? A hypocrite, imposing sentences for breaking the law when I myself broke the law? And here I am fantasizing about an affair with Windham, a married woman. Who am I, really? What am I? When the rules no longer apply, how do I categorize myself?

Dan pushed open the door to the church vestibule and encountered an usher of indeterminate gender, who had a buzz haircut but soft contours and gentle voice, no makeup, with a gold ring in the right ear. He had been told one earring served as a secret code to identify to other gays that this person was homosexual, but he couldn't remember whether the earring should be in the left or the right ear. Ashamed of his irreverent thoughts, Dan followed the usher up the aisle to a half-empty pew whose three inhabitants moved over to accommodate the newcomer. The person next to the aisle, who appeared to be an actual man, shared his hymnal with Dan, careful not to scrutinize him too closely. Picking up on this cue, Dan resisted his urge to scan the church to see whether he recognized anyone. Fixating on the page before him, he saw the same hymn sung in the black church. "I danced in the morning when the world was begun, and I danced in the moon and the stars and the sun, I danced for the scribe and the Pharisee, but they wouldn't dance, and they wouldn't follow me." He knew a scribe was a rules-bound bureaucrat, a Pharisee a politician who strictly adhered to Mosaic law, neither one able to dance in the spirit. Uptight. What was it other denominations said derisively about Episcopalians? God's frozen people. No wonder they didn't sing Lord of the Dance in the Anglican church.

He analyzed the ambience of St. Ignatius. Flowers and choir outstanding, no excess of furbelows and hoorah he would expect of a homosexual congregation. Not a piece of rococo in evidence. Walls, ceiling, and floor of old pine burnished to a golden sheen. Altar a table, upon which the single stained-glass window cast prismatic light. Pews resembled those found in country schools, no fancy cushions. From the corners of his eyes, Dan could see pairs of worshippers holding hands or resting arms across each other's shoulders. This was not in and of itself unusual, for such displays of affection were occasionally seen in his own church. But these pairs in St. Ignatius appeared to be same-sex, two women with mannish haircuts, two men with animated facial expressions more typical of heterosexual females. He expected to feel repulsion in the midst of these, but there was an innocence, a sincerity, a connectedness which touched his soul. Blest be the ties that bind. How often had he and Nora held hands in church? Not once that he could remember, after the obligatory handholding of their formal wedding ceremony in which they pledged to be faithful to each other until death did them part.

These gay people were forbidden the legal status of marriage which would validate their living arrangements, yet they reached out to touch each other, while he and Nora avoided such public sentiment. Why was this so? Were heterosexuals afraid nice people might surmise they also touched other body parts behind closed doors, those parts deemed unclean? Nasty, nasty, he remembered the mothers and grandmothers saying to children, mustn't touch. Yet he was compelled to peek inside the panties of girl cousins at family reunions when the adults weren't supervising. And he had performed furtive adolescent masturbation upon himself in the darkness of night when his longings overwhelmed him. What had caused him to want to violate girl rather than boy cousins? Had this been a deliberate, conscious decision on his part, a wish to

104

comply with societal rules which dictated he could only lust after the opposite sex? Or was this a form of predestination over which he had no control?

Why hadn't the worshippers at St. Ignatius been similarly inclined toward the opposite sex rather than being drawn in the direction of mirror images of themselves? Had they, at some developmental point, made a conscious decision to be perverse, engage in illegal conduct, become sodomizers rather than procreators? His mother, his aunts and grandmothers, had they forbidden their children to do things they themselves might have done, wished they could do, did do when no one was looking? Were women free from the lustful instincts which bedeviled men? He couldn't remember Nora making sex an imperative, but Windham seemed sensual to the marrow of her bones, despite her finessing his overtures on *Mandamus*, and he had known women who couldn't live without sex.

He simply could not make sense of it, the mysteries of sex, and here in this place, St. Ignatius the sanctuary of the despised, he suddenly was shocked by the audacity, the arbitrariness, of the law in decreeing certain sexual behaviors seemly and others unseemly, condemning some of Gods children, those attracted to Sameness rather than Otherness, to suffer public humiliation and fines and jail sentences. For decades, as an arm of the Court he had trod where only God should tread. How dare he! He had a sudden urge to rush into the street, stand on the corner of Sixth and Queen, and issue a public decree nullifying all sentences he had levied for crimes against nature.

As the congregation said the Invocation, "Write these words in our hearts, we beseech Thee, O God," Dan's face flushed with shame for his many trespasses against those whom only God should judge. He felt rage toward sanctimonious authority which invaded the privacy of everyone, decreeing which orifice could legitimately be stimulated by which appendage, who was approved to give and receive bodily fluids and who was not. Where had society's sexual voyeurism, sadism, begun? He felt certain this havoc had not been introduced by Jesus-in-Whom-God-is-Love, though Jesus' name had been coopted by the sex police. He was grateful when the Reverend Amanda Abingdon came forward from the front row and took her place at the podium which served as a pulpit, for the sight of her quieted his mounting rage. Her black cassock and white collar, and the respect she engendered in the faces of the congregation, were balm for his wounded soul. Her long, dark hair framed her heart-shaped face. Though she wore no visible makeup, her eyes were smoky and her

106

cheeks glowed with health. He felt stirrings of attraction toward her, momentarily imagined kissing her mouth where her teeth showed white between her pink lips. Had he met her at a gathering of spiritual leaders, unaware of her sexual orientation, he surely would have found an excuse to place his hand on her shoulder.

She spoke with a distinctly British accent unlike that of Peter Arnold. Dan felt excitement he had never found in St. Philip's. She had a way of putting things which stimulated his imagination rather than chilling his thought process. "We are come together in the fullness of this day, to rejoice over our good fortune being together in this place. May we open our hearts to all those who worship elsewhere, and they open their hearts to us, in the glory of God." Her voice was strong yet tender, with a sensual huskiness. The female ministers Dan had heretofore experienced—there was that legal jargon again—those allowed into the pulpit by the Episcopal male hierarchy, either were maternal or intellectual or sisterly or tinged with too many male hormones, without a hint of sex appeal. But this avowed lesbian in St. Ignatius' pulpit exuded a powerful, libidinous charisma similar to that of popular male preachers, the white Billy Grahams and black Sweet Daddy Graces, and also, he grudgingly acknowledged, charlatans like Jimmy Swaggart, who drew shipwrecked souls like finger mullet attracted bluefish.

Dan gladly dug into his pocket for a generous contribution when the basket was passed along his pew. He eagerly went forward to partake of Communion from the Common Cup, dismissing his fear of contracting AIDs. When the Reverend Abingdon placed her hand upon his head after he received the Elements, he felt a flood of warmth wash over him which was not completely due to the wine. After the Benediction, in which she proclaimed that the Word of God empowers us to speak and act, and the congregation responded we will dare to act as God directs, Dan exited the church in close proximity to his fellow worshippers, not minding that their arms brushed his. He realized he had not missed the de rigueur He and Him and Father and Son in the recitation of the Creed and the Lord's Prayer, the incantation of the Doxology. The changes in language had been unobtrusive: I believe in God the Almighty, Jesus Christ Child of God, Our Holy Parent. The gay church had succeeded In de-sexing the liturgy without the clumsiness of mainstream churches' token attempts at inclusivity. Hallelujah! Praise the Lord! He must come here again, soon, not out of curiosity, but from his own need for freedom and comfort.

As he shook the hand of the Reverend Abingdon, he did not wish to let it go. Thinking of his desire for Windham, he was on the verge of saying, if you believe homosexuals are discriminated against because you follow the path for which God created you, you should try being a heterosexual who breaks out of the straitjacket of traditional marital monogamy. But he was afraid he might startle her with his forthrightness, that somehow she might view adulterous heterosexual behavior as sinful, whereas—there was that jargon again—she had compassion for the illegal couplings of her fellow gays. He must convince her of the goodness of his heart before he revealed his own secret truth, for he did not want to be marginalized by this gay congregation the way his own church marginalized homosexuals. He wanted to be accepted, respected, yes, now he could admit to himself, he wanted to be loved, for his authentic self, heart, mind, body, and soul. As he looked into Reverend Abingdon's smoky eyes, he realized this was what he had always wanted, since he was a little boy, simply to be loved, no more than that, no less, because he was a child of God.

When he arrived home and saw Nora's Buick parked in the drive, he found himself looking for her rather than avoiding her. She was in the mud room in her gardening clothes, tidying up the shelves. "I want to tell you something," he said, "I'm sorry for what I said this morning. You're a good person. We're all good people, you and Windham Doubeck and Jackie Jerrold and me, getting through life the best we know how. If you want a divorce, you can have whatever property settlement you want, have your lawyer draw up the papers."

"There was a message for you on the machine when I got back from church," she said. "Clark says weather forecast is looking ominous. Said to check our hurricane supplies." She lined up the gas lamps, the water jugs. "We need new mantles for the lanterns, batteries for the radio. Shall I buy them, or will you?"

Dan lost his urge to connect with Nora on an emotional level. "All right, all right, I'll get ready for the big blow which will fizzle before it reaches land. Every year, Clark insists on performing this ritual."

"Better safe than sorry," Nora said.

Dan cut the engine. "Bad fog," he said. "No getting through the inlet until it dissipates. Let's lower the dinghy

110

and paddle in. Grab a bowl of seafood chowder at Tide's Edge Café and listen to oldies but goodies."

"Fog reminds me of Portland," said Windham.

"Where haven't you lived? I've hardly been out of Fearrington."

"Let's anchor here and nestle in the cabin until the fog lifts," said Windham.

"Aye, aye," said Dan, going forward to take the anchor from the hatch and run the line through the chock. Nestling in the cabin with Windham was an offer he didn't want to refuse. When he went down the ladder, he didn't find Windham in the cabin. Passing the galley, he slid open the door to the forward berth, and there she was, smiling at him from the V-shaped bed. "Come lie next to me," she said.

"Walk into my parlor, said the spider to the fly," said Dan. "And have you many a curious thing to show me?" He kicked off his shoes, positioning himself on the triangular bed with his bare feet pointing toward her head.

"You think I want to smell your stinky feet?" she asked.

"I think you best turn around and put your head next to mine in the aft end of the berth," he said. "These are cramped quarters." He pushed open the side windows.

"I rather like the proximity." She began rubbing her bare toes against his toes. "This is cozy." She pushed up her shirt and pointed to a scar beneath her right breast. "Here's a curious thing I can show you. Can you guess what it is?"

Dan gently ran his forefinger across the scar. "Hope you haven't had silicone implants," he said.

Windham laughed. "It's where I clumsily sliced myself with a fish knife. Took ten stitches."

"I can do better than that." Dan shoved his waistband below his navel. "See there?" He pointed to a scar on the left side of his abdomen. "Hernia. Sixteen stitches. Not fun."

Windham sat up and removed her shirt. She bent forward. "You see that place where my spine curves to one side and then back again?" Dan stroked her spine, resisting the impulse to cup his hand around her breast. "Scoliosis," she said. "Diagnosed when I was fourteen.

Thought I'd have to have a rod implant, but the condition arrested by the time I was in high school."

"Darn, I thought you were perfect," Dan said. He held up one leg and wriggled his toes. "You see that bulge on the side of my big toe? Bunion."

Windham rolled from the bed and pulled off her shorts and bikini bottom, exposing her buttocks. "Look closely," she said, "and you'll see a line of small scars shaped like a scimitar. Chickenpox. When I was seven."

Dan sat up and kissed the scimitar. "No weapon formed against thee shall prosper," he said.

Windham turned around. "What?"

"Quote from the Bible," said Dan. "Isaiah."

She sat back down on the bed. "I didn't take you for a Bible-thumper."

Dan put his arms around her, feeling the warmth of her body against his. "I'm not," he said. "I'm about to break a commandment and commit adultery with you, if you'll allow me."

"I won't just allow you, I'll enable," said Windham. She french-kissed him as she relieved him of his pants. Then she kissed his adam's apple, his chest, his hernia scar.

"I don't know whether I can perform," said Dan. "I'm not a young guy. Been a long time."

"Shut up and do what comes naturally," Windham murmured. "I won't tell anyone if you won't."

Afterward, they lay together listening to the waves lap at the hull of the boat. Dan had forgotten how relaxing coitus could be, how restorative. Making love with a woman who enjoys making love was more fulfilling than being appointed Chief Judge of Superior Court, being elected Commodore of the Fearrington Yacht Club. He understood why the Duke of Windsor renounced the throne of England for Wallis Simpson. Dan's dread of old age began to evaporate, replaced with anticipation of good things to come. The ache inside him, which had existed ever since he lost Toby, subsided. He would give up his kingdom to lie forever on this oddly-shaped bed with Windham, in the land where the bong-tree grows.

"I'm hungry," said Windham. "Let's put the dinghy down. I could use some chowder."

114

"Me, too," said Dan. "But first I want you to tell me something. What exactly do you do up at Mount Gilead with that organization Grassroots?"

"I'll tell you if you promise to keep it confidential."

"Good lord, is it some sort of skulduggery?"

"I tape interviews, on the QT. Employers don't know about it. Think I'm some sort of Spanish to English translator."

"What's your focus, low wages? Poor housing? Child labor?"

"Dan, I'm an investigative reporter on a grant from the University of California School of Journalism. Long-range project. Will be broadcast on public television when it's completed."

"Like I said, what's your focus?"

"Sexual exploitation of female migrant workers. Rape. Happens all the time in the fields. I interview the victims."

"Good god."

"Can't tell you more. Maybe after it's all put together. For now, let's go get some chowder."

They paddled in and beached the dinghy on the stubble of peat and oyster shells which rimmed the inlet. "Making love brings up an appetite," he said.

"So does smoking pot," said Windham.

"I wouldn't know," said Dan.

"Truth is," said Windham, "pot isn't part of Peter's and my lives. Back when we were in high school, yes. A phase, peer pressure. Cuando yo era un nino yo pensaba como nino."

"Qwando what? Me no speaka da Spanish."

"When I was a child, I thought as a child. But when I grew up I put away childish things."

"Now you're quoting the Bible. First Corinthians," said Dan.

"So I am. I'm not a heathen. I'm a spiritual person. But not a church mouse." Windham took hold of his hand. "Shhh, be quiet," she whispered. In the few moments it had taken for them to reach shore, the fog had thickened so they could barely make out each other's faces. They stood without speaking at the edge of the sea until they began to sink up to their ankles in muck. Giggling at the sucking sound their feet made, they disengaged and headed slowly in the direction of the café on higher ground. They could hear the cries of gulls. "If you are gone too soon," Windham breathed into Dan's ear, "I shall walk upon the shore, follow the beach to its farthest reach, howl silently at the moon."

"Where'd you get that?"

Windham squeezed his hand. "I made it up."

"You lie. Nobody can make up a poem that good that quick, except maybe Walt Whitman."

"It's easy. Anybody can do it, if you're in touch with the world around you and your true feelings. Children do it all the time, speak in rhyme." She clapped her hands together. "I know what! Let's be children again in the fog." She twirled around and around until she grew dizzy and fell against him. They locked arms around each other's waists and crab-walked through the ever-thickening fog which was soft on their faces, stuck out their tongues to scoop the fog into their mouths like cotton candy. In the damp, muffled silence, Dan and Windham and the fog and the sand and the sea seemed the same state of being.

Dan's long legs took him slightly ahead of Windham, so she had to quicken her steps to keep up with him. Suddenly he pitched forward over an obstacle obscured by the fog. Windham also fell forward as a squeal went up from the large animal object underfoot. "Nora!" Dan shouted in disbelief.

The man straddling Nora grunted his displeasure, but Dan ignored him. "Nora, my god! What are you doing here like this?"

The man lifted himself off Nora. "You should know the public access law," drawled the man, "for you be de judge."

"Jackie Jerrold!"

Jackie faced Dan, his pants at half-mast around his knees. "Anything below the high tide line is free territory," he said. "Your wife, she's on the beach below the high tide line. And salvage law of the sea says finders keepers."

Dan could make out Jackie in the hazy sunlight filtering through the fog. His features were pugnacious, like a bully in the school yard. His penis was still partially erect. Sunlight glinted off a tiny metallic ring inserted in his foreskin. Good god, why would a man mutilate himself so savagely? Even the young, well-toned surfers who communally showered at the Club, sporting tattoos on their bronze bodies, didn't wear genital jewelry. Yet middle-aged Jackie Jerrold had a penis ring. And it had been up inside Nora, for god's sake! How could she bear the pain if it nicked her, when for years she'd been sensitive about any thrusting during intercourse? "Nora, are you insane?" Dan babbled. "What if someone sees you like this? What if you get arrested?" He seized her slacks from the sand and tossed them to her. Then he sniffed the fog-shrouded air. "Pot!" he shouted, "you've been smoking pot!"

Nora sat up, brushing sand from her shoulders. "I feel just fine," she said. "Better than I've felt in years."

Windham stood off to one side, calmly regarding Jackie's penis. "That's amazing," she said.

"Like having your ear pierced," said Jackie.

"Jackie's younger than Dan," volunteered Nora.

"Why in hell do you wear that dingle-dangle in your dick?" Dan demanded, unintentionally engaging in alliteration.

119

Jackie pulled his pants up and fastened them. "I do it to piss off guys like you, when you find out I'm fucking your wife."

Dan threw a punch at Jackie, who sidestepped him. Whirling around, Dan threw another punch. This one landed, knocking Jackie backward into the water. The two men growled, wrestling at the tide's edge and tumbling over each other. They rolled into the fog, out of view of Nora and Windham.

"You want to fight?" Nora asked Windham. "I'm game if you are." She seized Windham's ponytail. "I hate your goddamn hair!"

The two women fell onto the sand, scrambled to their feet, fell again, rolling over and over as they tried to maintain a grip on each other. Suddenly the fog began to lift and rays of sunlight broke through. Forms reshaped themselves. The illumination brought hostilities to a halt. Dan and Jackie sloshed toward Windham and Nora, who were covered in sand from head to toe, like chickens dredged for frying. Dan reached for Windham and Jackie reached for Nora, dousing the women in the sea to remove the sand.

Nora slipped away from Jackie and lunged for Dan. "You sonofabitch!" She pushed his shoulders down until he began to submerge. Struggling out of her grasp, he dived deep to seize her ankles and drag her beneath the surface.

"Come on," Jackie said to Windham. "Let's go get a cup of java while they settle their issues. My marriage therapy is over for the day."

"I swear to god," said Windham as she shook salt water from her hair, "I couldn't believe my ears when Dan called Nora's name. What are the odds we would run into you?"

"My house is just over the dunes," said Jackie. "Nora dropped by, fog rolled in, and I didn't want to miss a chance like this to fuck on the beach with a judge's wife. Too bad she got found out by her prick of a husband. But she doesn't owe him a thing. What's sauce for the goose...." Jackie pulled a plastic bag out of his pants pocket and extracted a joint and a zippo lighter. "You smoke?" he asked as he lit up. Windham took a toke. "I knew it," said Jackie.

"Knew what?"

"What Nora told me, you being from California, I figured you don't use hemp just for rigging." He offered Windham another toke. "Beats the hell outta that booze they scarf down at the Club. This won't give you cirrhosis, won't get you a DWI." Jackie tamped off the joint and zipped it back up in the bag. "Let's not be selfish," he said. "Let's share the wealth. I got a feeling de judge won't be so judgmental after Nora gets finished with him. She's not a bad chick. Only needed some tuning up after spending most of her life with that stuffed shirt."

"Dan's not a bad dude," said Windham.

"Dude," said Jackie. "You talk like that with de judge?"

Windham laughed. "Cuando en Roma."

"When in Rome. I know Spanish, use it all the time when I'm in Miami. I'm not the dumbass people here take me for."

"I don't think you're a dumbass," said Windham. "I think you're a rebel, an iconoclast. Maybe an anarchist." She looked over her shoulder and saw Dan in close conversation with Nora.

"Takes one rebel to know another one," said Jackie. "I hear through the Nora grapevine you're doing a migrant thing up at Mount Gilead. Sock it to those assholes who run the pickle plant. It's like a plantation, bourbon-soaked masters and jalapeno-chomping slaves. Time somebody cleaned their clock."

"You're an anomaly."

"How so?"

"You're a counter-culture capitalist with the soul of a socialist."

"And you party at the Club like an aristocrat though you work saving downtrodden immigrants." Jackie turned to glance at Dan and Nora. "For now, I've enough on my hands dealing with the Queen of the DAR. I'm becoming rather fond of her. Though as a diagnosed sociopath, I usually just seize my opportunities and avoid commitments."

"Know thyself," said Windham. "And I know I'm more than fond of her husband."

Jackie and Windham were well into their chowder when Nora and Dan joined them at the café. "That looks delicious," said Nora, peering into Windham's bowl. "I want some."

Dan couldn't believe his ears. "You want fish chowder?"

"Oh my yes."

When the chowder arrived, Dan watched Nora out of the corners of his eyes as she crumbled oyster crackers, squirted Tabasco, and ate spoonful after spoonful of the stew. All tension seemed to have left her. "Fog came up so suddenly," said Windham. "Is that common around here?"

"Happens," said Jackie. "Thing I like about living here, never know what the weather's going to do. Bright and sunny, then it rains. Rains, then a blue sky. Changeable, especially when a hurricane's skulking around in the Atlantic. I get bored with the same-old."

"What's up with Flossie?" asked Dan.

"Last I checked, looked like it's a goner."

"I told your Uncle Clark," Dan said to Windham, "not to get his Hobarts in a twist over this storm. He overreacts."

"Didn't overreact to Hurricane Hazel," said Windham. "He was the last one to evacuate, car up to the hubcaps in sound water when we crossed over the bridge. I was a terrified little girl. Maybe Hazel was a lesson for him to be more judicious."

Nora giggled. "Judicious! That's Dan's prerogative."

Jackie took out the half-smoked marijuana joint and offered it to Dan. "How 'bout a toke?"

"Hell no," said Dan, looking around. "Not in public. I may be retired, but I still have a certain amount of propriety." He kept waiting for Nora to make her pilgrimage to the bathroom to throw up the meal she had just eaten. But she was enjoying herself in the company of her new lover, her husband, and her husband's lover. What did he and Nora have now? An open marriage? It was one thing to commit adultery in secret, but in the presence of one's spouse, this somehow seemed perverse. He was seeing a Nora he never knew existed, more akin to the young debutante who eagerly succumbed to his carnal desires when they were engaged, than to the proper matron who

125

was mother of their son and a model of ladylike comportment for other Fearrington wives.

Nora leaned against Jackie's shoulder and patted Windham on the arm from time to time. Her behavior was stranger than the sudden fog. She got up from her seat. "Excuse me," she said. Dan knew she'd head for the door cutely marked Gulls, next to the door marked Buoys, so she could throw up her meal, but instead, she went over to the juke box. "Anybody got quarters?" she called out.

Jackie fished in his sodden pockets and laid three coins on the table. Nora scooped them up, inserted them into the juke box, and punched in her selections. A gospel song came over the sound system. That figures, religious music, thought Dan, until he heard the lyrics as Nora sang along with the music, affecting a mountain twang, "A man is tinder...a woman is fire...and the devil is a mighty wind...." Jackie Jerrold joined in.

"Since when did you take up country music?" he asked his wife. "I thought you hated that stuff."

"Since you got out of the house and went to live on your boat," said Nora. "Daniel, honey, I've taken up a lot of things since you took up with Windham. I'm thinking about taking up belly-dancing."

126

"But you haven't got the belly for it!" Dan immediately regretted his sarcasm.

Nora's happy mood abruptly changed to bitterness. "I had a fine belly," she said. "Before Toby had his accident." She came back to sit next to Jackie, and the light went out of her eyes.

"Tell me about your son Toby," said Windham.

"Don't go there," said Jackie.

Nora lifted her chin defiantly. "I can belly dance at the community center on Thursday nights. They give lessons."

"Today's Wednesday," said Dan inanely.

"What I love is the veils and the bangles," said Nora.

"The dingles and the dangles," muttered Dan.

"The bright colors, way the skirts swirl. I'm making a costume will knock your eyes out. Jackie's helping me put it together."

"Nora's quite graceful," Jackie said.

"At Carolina she was the best dancer at Germans," said Dan, "like Cyd Charisse."

Nora's face lit up. "Why, Daniel," she said, "I didn't think you remembered."

"'Bout time for me to exit this love fest," said Jackie.

"Hey diddle diddle, how's this for a riddle?" Nora did sing-song. "What's pot got that liquor's not?"

Dan sighed and stood up. "I'll sign for the tab." He held out his hand to Windham.

Nora waved goodbye. "Ta-ta. See you 'round the Club."

Reds

When the red warning flag is flown, ocean

conditions are dangerous to swimmers,

who should immediately exit the water.

Rule 23

Fearrington Yacht Club Handbook

"**W**e gave the sheet a hard pull," Bill was saying, "didn't use the jenny."

"What you need is a Morgan Out-Island," said Clark. "Nine thousand pounds of lead in the keel, for a low center of gravity."

"Been thinking, Perkins diesel's a honey."

Clark took Bill's glass. "Let me get you another one. Jerianne's heading our way." He made a beeline for the bar, where Dan leaned on the counter, his eyes fixed on the overhead television set.

"Hate to admit it," said Dan, "but this next storm might be the big blow. Flossie fizzled like I thought it would. Look at that weather map, here comes another one."

"I told you to lay In supplies," said Clark. "Going to get a big one this year. Been feeling it in the air for weeks."

"Fishing's not much," said Dan. "Brought in a few spots, couple speckled trout, puppy drum."

"I could use a trout if you want to let loose of one."

Dan slid off the stool. "Got 'em on ice. I'll pick you out a good one, put it on the lower shelf in the cooler. Don't forget it when you leave."

"I can wait," said Clark. "Don't trouble yourself."

"No trouble. At my advanced age, I have to do things when I think of them, before they slip my mind."

Bullshit, he said to himself as he went down the steps to the lower deck. You just want an excuse to see whether Windham and Peter have arrived. You hope she shows up because you can't stand not being with her, and then you go crazy when she's here because you have to pretend to be casual, discreet, keep your distance, not embarrass Nora. Everyone suspects you and Windham have a thing, and Nora and Jackie are no secret. Why the hell do we play this hypocritical game?

Passing the open doors to the ballroom, he heard the voice of the bingo caller. "Twelve dollars for the worst card. Loser gets to be a winner." Dan glanced through the

132

doors at the throng of members hunched over rows of long tables covered with blue bingo cards. At the front of the room, the caller spun a wire basket and withdrew a number. "G 59." A groan went up from several players. Another spin. "N 43." More groans. Grandparents and parents leaned over the boards of their progeny. Teenagers worked several boards at a time. The overhead fans whirred. This is what the Club's really about, thought Dan. Families having fun together. Regattas are only window-dressing. If Nora and I had grandchildren, we'd be in there with them, cheering them on, celebrating when they won a few bucks and a Snickers bar. But the McInnes name stops with me, since Toby died without issue. Without issue. There he went again. How long would it take for him to purge himself of legalese? First we kill all the lawyers, wrote Shakespeare in Henry the Sixth. Not a bad idea.

He walked toward the kitchen. Rocking chairs were lined up along the porch railing. In his mind's eye he saw now long-gone female McInneses in the chairs, summer dresses damp with salt moisture and perspiration, sleeping babies in their arms, waiting for the end of day and the long ride back to town with empty picnic baskets. The Club was a good place. He loved it here. He was grateful to the competitive, gregarious, aristocratic sailors who had founded this club a hundred and fifty years earlier as a watering hole, a haven from wind and sun, and passed membership down to succeeding generations. It was easy to spot who was related to whom. Sharp or pug noses, short or tall stature, bow legs, knock knees, curly or straight hair, large or small bottoms, old and young of the same family. Toby no doubt had emanated from Dan's loins, with a bit of Nora mixed in. Had they a daughter, she would have been a copy of Nora with an unmistakable strain of McInnes.

Why had it begun to annoy him that no blacks were among the membership, no Jews, no one other than closely-related white-bread Protestants? There was an upside to homogeneity. Less friction, everyone doing things the same way. No nappy hair in washbasins, no soul food in the kitchen, no rap music at teenage dances. No invitations to a bris or a bar mitzvah, no menorahs, no dreidels on the dining porch. At Club socials, "Hey, how ya'll doin', doin' fine, come see us," instead of, "Whazzup, my man, keep it cool, dude." A comfort zone, the only cultural problem the generation gap, bridged when teenagers matured into membership on their own recognizance. Own recognizance, there it was again, the legal jargon. Retirement had not deleted it from his brain.

As he placed the trout in the large cooler in the kitchen, he surveyed the containers of food on the communal shelves. There was something comforting about the platters of fried chicken and ham biscuits, bowls of potato salad, dessert dishes piled with chess tarts, pitchers of minted iced tea. All his life he had seen the same food in the Club kitchen, tried-and-true recipes passed down from mother to daughter to granddaughter. If the Club embraced diversity, this would have to change. Strange condiments would appear, matzo balls sizzling in deep-fat cookers, tacos everywhere, smell of soy sauce In the air. Much as he hated to admit it, ever since the civil rights activity of the 1960s he missed having black cooks washing dishes, black nannies minding babies in the nursery, the black bartender who kept everyone's secrets, the black porter who toted heavy beach bags and ice chests out to the cars. The preppy young white staff who now attended to these matters lacked the courtesy and deference which had given the Club its own grace. How could he feel this way, ambivalent about the loss of privilege in the advent of egalitarianism? His racist yet pious great-aunt Sally In the nursing home conceded before she died that segregation likely was wrong in God's eyes. "I guess the Nigras are the same as us," she reasoned, "but when I was a girl I was taught their brains are smaller and they need us to direct them, and I'm too old to learn any different."

Was he also a dog too old to learn new tricks? Apparently not, for he was learning a great deal since meeting Windham. Now he felt split, part of him in the new way of being, part of him stuck in the old. Was his discomfort the consequence of Original Sin? Having tasted of the fruit of the tree of knowledge, he was no longer able to rest in blissful ignorance when he violated the Golden Rule. He was painfully aware of the schism between the honorable gentleman he had purported to be, and the hypocrite he actually was. As he recrossed the porch on his way back upstairs to the bar, his heart cried out, oh Windham, please come to the Club tonight, please, so I am not alone with my confusion. His prayer was answered when Windham suddenly appeared with Peter and greeted him in that teasing way she had, innocence in her eyes, an enigmatic smile on her lips. The threesome mounted the stairs together. "Caught a rip tide this afternoon," said Peter.

"First thing alerts us a hurricane might be coming our way," said Dan. "Yellow warning flag on the lifeguard stand replaced by one red flag with a black square in the center, means watch out for tropical storm force winds. Two red flags signal the hurricane is upon us." When they reached the upper deck, Dan gestured toward the ocean. "Long time before a storm strikes, start getting these rips. No problem for surfers, but swimmers can be in bad trouble. A rip's sneaky, below the smooth surface, hard to detect with the naked eye. That's why we put out warning flags." Sneaky, thought Dan, like a con artist who charms you until he's got you ensnared in his grip. Jackie Jerrold and Nora.

Clark joined them and talked animatedly. I'm taking bets when this new one, Mariah, will hit. We'll be in the bull's eye."

Windham seemed surprised. "I thought you said we had nothing to worry about. Blue sky, green sea, light air, all is calm."

"Calm before the storm," said Dan. "Let's get an update." He walked with Windham and Peter to the bar.

"What is the life of cyclones in this part of the world?" asked Peter.

"Hurricanes," said Windham.

"Season starts in June, peaks in September, ends in November. Our storms usually form in southern Atlantic or Caribbean, go west and north, parallel the coast." Dan surveyed the bottles arranged at the back of the bar. "What's your pleasure?"

"Rum," said Peter. "A Black Rat."

"Doesn't sound appetizing," said Dan.

"Aussie for rum and cola," said Windham. "Hispanics call it Cuba Libre, with lime."

Dan pointed to Bacardi and held up three fingers for the bartender. "Storms start as tropical depressions, maximum winds under 33 knots. We get a bunch of those each season, hard to predict which might turn dangerous." He handed the rum drinks to Windham and Peter.

Clark Doubeck said, "Wind speed increases in center, pressure drops, keeps falling as wind increases. Hurricane can be up two hundred miles wide, maximum wind speed over two hundred. When it strikes, a day of battering, eerie calm with blue sky when the eye passes, then storm takes a second bite on your ass even stronger than before."

138

Windham listened intently as Dan continued. "Trick is guessing which storms will come inland, which veer offshore. We used to be at their mercy, but now we get pretty good advance information before they make landfall."

Nora suddenly appeared. "They're destroying the nest!" she said. "We've got to stop them." She ran out of the bar, across the upper deck, down the stairs toward the dunes, waving her hands. "Stop it!" she shouted. "Stop it right now."

Unused to seeing Nora McInnes so animated, Club members leaned over the porch railing and watched her push through the sea oats until she reached three children digging in the sand. When they ignored her, she seized one boy and jerked him to a standing position, berating him.

Clark Doubeck put a hand on Dan's shoulder. "You better go after her. The parents of those kids could make a real fuss."

By the time Dan reached Nora, the three children were running toward one of the nearby cottages, and she was kneeling in the sand smoothing out the children's footprints with the palms of her hands. "Selfish little brats," she muttered.

"For god's sake, keep your voice down," said Dan. "Everyone's watching. What's got into you?"

"Somebody has to protect the turtles." Nora pointed to a small emblem on her collar which spelled Turtle Watch Corps. "I've joined up. As a volunteer." She reached into the sea oats and pulled out wooden stakes entwined with orange rope. "Against the law to disturb the nesting site. Five hundred dollar fine for violating the ordinance."

"How could a bunch of little kids know there's a turtle nest here?" asked Dan. "What the hell difference does it make? Nesting season's over."

Nora untangled the stakes from the rope. "The mother turtle will come back to this same place to lay her eggs next season," she said. "If she finds the nest disturbed, all her effort for nothing. She'll drag her great body up the beach in the moonlight." Nora jammed a stake deep into the sand.

"Sea turtle tracks," said Dan. "look like a Marine tank came ashore."

"The Corps marked off the nest and put up a warning sign," said Nora. "Very clearly marked." She moved several feet and jammed down another stake.

"Nora," said Dan, "I've been trying not to mention this, way things are with us, but there's something gone wrong with you. You obsess about rules and regulations. Now you're obsessing about measuring sea turtle nests. You need to talk to a doctor."

She lunged at him, shoving him backward into sea oats. He winced when he felt a cactus penetrate the seat of his trousers. Nora kicked sand at him. "You bastard!" she screamed. "You don't care about turtle babies. Well, I do! I do! This is my nest. I'm assigned to watch over it, protect the babies from harm. Such tiny creatures when they're born. With such a long journey ahead of them." She sank onto the sand, wrapped her arms about herself. "Goddamn you!" She choked on tears. "You didn't love Toby. You just needed him to help you sail your goddamn boat. You never thought about his safety. Catch the wind, win the race, that's what counted. When the boom slammed him into the water, you didn't try to save him. He was unconscious, and you let him drown."

Dan saw a throng of Club members leaning over the rail as Clark made his way down the steps toward the dunes. Dan gestured to Clark to stay away, and he started back up the steps, waving his arms to signal members to go back to their socializing. "I didn't let Toby drown," Dan said. "We were in the middle of a race. We were endangering other boats. Before I could go after him, I had to maneuver.."

Nora wiped her eyes with sandy fingers. "You sanctimonious bastard. You sacrificed our child so you could play hero to the other yachtsmen. Who did you think you were? Abraham and Isaac? So what if a couple of boats got smashed? A few tubes of fibreglass, some coats of paint, but nothing could bring Toby back. Nothing." Tears flooded her cheeks.

"He was my son, too. He would have carried on the McInnes name." Dan knelt on the sand, burying his head in his arms. His body shook. He forced himself to face Nora. This was the first time since Toby's death he had allowed his eyes to look directly into hers. What he saw broke his heart. Her eyes were murky gray, like the sea when a front moves in, oceans of despair in a thin, aging face. Twelve years had passed since they put Toby into the grave beside his great-grandfather Tobias McInnes.

142

Their life together had been in irons, stalled. One Club season had followed another. Christmases without merriment had come and gone. Toby's sailing trophies gathered dust in his bedroom, where his Woodberry Forest prep school jacket still lay folded neatly on his bed. And here was Nora, holding Toby in her heart, refusing to let him go. How many times had Dan turned away from her when she began a conversation which indirectly referred to their son? How often had he pretended not to hear her complain about the aches and pains in the vicinity of her womb?

"I wanted more children," Nora was saying, "even if it meant risking a Mongoloid. We could have afforded a special-needs child. The doctor said the odds would be in our favor. But you didn't want to touch me any more. Not after we lost Toby. Stop staring at me. Say something to me, please."

Sound formed inside Dan, from a place deeper and darker than the bottom of the ocean, rose higher and higher, into his chest, his throat, until he couldn't breathe. He turned his face toward the sunset and made noises over which he had no control, animal sounds he couldn't form into words. He was speaking in tongues, like the Pentecostals. This was what it must be like for a defendant in his courtroom, not understanding the coded lawyer-speak incomprehensible to ordinary people. He wrapped his arms around Nora, weeping until the light went out of the sky. When he could form words, he murmured into her shoulder, "Of course I wanted you. Of course. You are my wife, the mother of our child. But how could you want me? My carelessness took Toby from you, our child you worked so long to conceive and bear. You never got to see him into manhood. Nora, I couldn't forgive myself. How could I ask you to forgive me?"

Nora smoothed his hair, causing sand to fall into his eyes. "I don't throw up any more," she said. "And I've quit shoplifting."

Dan wasn't sure he'd heard her right. "You've quit what?"

"I did it for years, right under your nose. But you never noticed."

"I would have bought you anything you wanted," said Dan. "You could just charge to our credit cards."

"Stealing was something I had to do. I don't know how to explain it. Something I could do for myself. Take things without anybody knowing."

144

"What if you got caught? Wife of a judge. From a good family. Newspaper would have had a field day. Nobody would have invited us to dinner, afraid you'd walk off with the silver."

"I was smart," she said. "Nobody knew."

"What did you steal? Do we have any stolen property in our house? We must dispose of it immediately. Now that I know, I'm complicit if I don't turn you in." Complicit. There it was again, the legal jargon.

"Clothes, mostly. I didn't bring my loot home. Kept it in my Club locker." She laughed. "Not my regular locker. The one on the other side of the shower stalls. I never used the things I stole, left them in the shopping bags. Knowing I had them stowed in my locker made me feel better."

"Is that why the Club keeps charging me for lockers 73 and 14 in the ladies' dressing room? I couldn't figure that out, why you needed two lockers to hold a towel and suntan lotion."

"Why didn't you ask me about the charge?"

"Afraid of hearing the answer, I suppose. Remember Al Patterson? He kept two lockers in the men's dressing room, one where he stashed his whiskey because his wife supervised him at the upstairs bar. He'd stand there in his swim trunks, taking a snort before he went out on the beach. We all pretended not to notice."

Dan glanced toward the Club. The porch lights had come on. "Do you want me to stop seeing Windham? I'll do whatever you say. I owe you that much."

"You owe me? I don't want to be a debt you have to pay."

"Didn't mean it to sound like that."

"Would giving up Windham mean I'd have to stop seeing Jackie?"

"Of course. Seems only fair."

"Then I don't give a damn what you do with Windham. Actually, I rather like her. She's how I would've been if I hadn't lived in Fearrington all my life. If I hadn't married you."

"God pity us both," said Dan. "Of all sad words of tongue or pen, the saddest are these, it might have been."

He was silent for a moment, then, "You're one helluva gal." Why did I tell her this, he thought, it sounds hollow, patronizing, but I really mean it.

"Yes, I am," said Nora. "Jackie Jerrold made me realize this. He likes being with me. We have fun."

"Are you in love with him? I don't mean to be critical, especially with my feet of clay, but I don't see how.... You know he's from the wrong side of the tracks."

Nora stood up. "Exactly right. Jackie is, as we aristocrats say, common. Not born to the purple. White trash, my mother would call him if she were still alive. And that's why he's a tonic." She twisted the hair at the nape of her neck, the way she used to do when Dan was courting her. "Of course I'm not in love with Jackie Jerrold! I don't have to be. He's my hack-around buddy, my friend. He's taught me even us old gals can kick up our heels."

Dan reached out and took hold of her hand. She didn't pull away. "I think I'm jealous," he said. "Can't stand the thought of him putting his...dingle dangle...into you."

"Serves you right," said Nora. She let go of his hand. "I don't think we need give the Club any more entertainment tonight. Race you to the parking lot!" She took off running

147

through the sea oats, Dan stumbling along behind her, only slightly discomfited by the cactus spines embedded in his pants.

On November 17, Mariah prepared to strike. At eight on Friday morning, her center shifted west. By midday, two red flags with black square centers were displayed on the lifeguard stand, and evacuation had been ordered for all low-lying coastal areas. By five in the evening, the Fearrington Yacht Club Hurricane Hardies were in full swing at the bar, listening to Weather-One broadcast receivers, comparing tracking charts, fortifying themselves with alcohol. "Where the hell is Clark?" asked Bill. "Last I saw him, he was clearing out his locker."

"You know Clark," said Dan, "better safe than sorry. I'm on my way to move *Mandamus* to sheltered mooring."

"Can I lend a hand?"

"No thanks. Taken care of."

"Stop by when you're done," said Bill. "We might ride this one out."

"You're a damn fool. You want Jerianne to have to cash in your life insurance so she can support your brood?"

"That nigger from Chicago made a speech he's thinking of running for President. Saw it on CNN." Bill chuckled and went back to drinking gin.

By the time Dan and Windham had gotten under way in *Mandamus*, the channel was rolling with swells. He started the engine, but it fizzled. He tried again, and it died. "Damn thing's useless when you want it," said Dan. "What the hell. This is a sailboat, not a motorboat. We've plenty of wind." He hoisted the sails. "We can make a run for it. Before the worst gets here. I want to moor her in the safety of the marina for this big blow."

The wind shifted. "Watch it," Dan yelled, "I'm coming about." He headed into the wind. "Hard-a-lee!"

"You'll have to handle this," Windham said. "I'm chicken. Going below."

"Worst place you can be in a storm. You'll get seasick."

"I'll take my chances."

149

The sky went black. Rain came from nowhere, pounding Dan like birdshot. Wind whistled through the shrouds. The boat rode up a swell, headed down the slope. "I'm turning back to the Club!" Dan shouted to Windham. "Don't want to take a chance with you as my precious cargo."

By the time *Mandamus* made the Club dock, lightning was flashing and wind was tearing at the sails. "I'm going to batten down the hatches," said Dan. "You run for it, take shelter in the boathouse."

"I'll be damned," shouted Windham. She grabbed the halyard. "We're in this together. I'm with you all the way."

"Ought to anchor her in the channel, so she won't get the hell beat out of her against the dock. Too dangerous to ride this one out, and we'd never make it to shore in the dinghy in this gale." Dan worked quickly. "I'll put slack in the lines, hope the surge doesn't break her loose."

Disembarking, they almost lost their balance on the heaving dock. They ran through the pelting rain to the boathouse, using both pairs of hands to pull the door open and tug it closed after they were safely inside. Drenched with rain, Windham stood next to Dan and listened to the storm raging outside. "You think we can make it to the mainland in your car? What if the bridge is under water, like it was in Hazel?"

"Too late," said Dan. "Better off here until it's passed. We'll be flooded, that's for sure. Ocean and sound meet when a hurricane strikes this island dead on."

Windham appeared bewildered. "You mean we'll be trapped in here? We might drown?"

Dan pushed his wet hair out of his eyes. "We need to get ourselves a couple more feet off the ground." He climbed the boat racks to a dinghy. "Come on up." He reached down to Windham. Hours later, as salt water seeped into the boathouse and wind pounded the walls, Dan and Windham were snug on life jackets lining the cockpit, a tarp pulled over them for warmth. Dan removed his sweater and rolled it into a pillow. "In a few hours, the first round will be over and we'll be in the eye," he said. "Then we'll have, oh, maybe a half hour to get to the mainland before the back side of Mariah hits."

Windham was shivering. "Warm me up. I'm wet to my bones."

Dan removed their wet clothing and hung it on the boat rack. "We're two bugs in a rug," he said, snuggling next to her under the tarp.

"I'm still cold."

Dan put his arms around her, and she relaxed against him, her breath quickening as she heard his heart pounding. He kissed her, sweetly and gently at first, then deeply. "I want you more than anything I've ever wanted in my life," he said.

"You've got me, Babe." Windham gave herself to him, loving his weight upon her, not caring whether the dinghy might slip from its berth and crash onto the concrete floor below, whether the water rose to cover them.

"I'm Noah and you're Mrs. Noah and we're in the Ark," said Dan. "When the Flood recedes, the world will begin again."

They made love, slept, and made love again. Suddenly the wind died and the sound of rain ceased. They put on their clothes and waded out of the boathouse to Dan's car in the Club parking lot, managing to get the doors open as water seeped into the interior. Dan turned the key in the ignition, and yelled "Yes!" when the engine started up. The car plowed through the water covering the road, and they made it across the bridge over the channel. When they reached the drawbridge at the intracoastal waterway, a police car blocked the entrance. Recognizing Dan, the policeman waved him on, shouting as they passed.

"What did he say?" asked Windham.

"Get the hell outta here, you horse's ass!"

They got the hell out, reached the Holiday Inn before the far side of Mariah struck. Huddled in the dark dining room with other refugees, they dozed listening to the wind and rain bring Fearrington to its knees. In the bright blue morning, they wandered about ravaged streets, waded through deep puddles, awed by the destruction, watched people pick through debris. Jaycees offered hot coffee from the back of a van. Someone gave them jelly donuts. Dan's car started up again, and he flashed his beach resident pass at the National Guardsman who monitored ingress to the storm-ravaged island. "Gotta find my boat," Dan explained.

The guard leaned into the driver's window. "Watch out for live power lines. Down all over the place." He waved Dan on.

As his car bumped across the drawbridge, Dan put his left hand out of the window and pointed straight down with his index finger. "Beneath us is my great-grandfather's yacht," he told Windham. "The *Minnehaha*. Not a big boat, only nineteen feet, but with eight-foot beam and bowsprit twelve feet over cut-water. Built in New York by Bob Fish. She wasn't a thing of beauty, but the only contest she ever lost was with the Great Storm of 1899, floated her out of her boathouse, took her north, slammed her into this trestle. What's left of her has been here ever since, sunk in the muck. Like me, never left Fearrington, stuck in the muck." Bumping off the bridge onto the causeway, Dan slowed to ten miles an hour to weave through the downed telephone poles and fallen oaks.

"How do you know what your great-grandfather's boat looked like?" asked Windham. "Way before your time."

"You're not well versed on Club sailing families, are you? We pass our sea stories down through the generations. Best race *Minnehaha* won was in 1886, July Fourth regatta. Wind from the south with a brisk tide rising. Great-Granpa McInnes—they called him Great Scot, for obvious reasons—came in with a running time of one hour, forty-two minutes, forty seconds."

"Never been much into measuring things," said Windham. "More interested in quality than quantity."

"I could say something wicked, but I won't."

"Good God, look!" Windham rose in her seat and leaned out the passenger window. Furniture haphazardly lined the causeway, tables piled on mattresses piled on chairs, rugs and lamps heaped here and there. A broken surfboard made a V against an overturned boat trailer. Beneath cottages where walls once stood, she could see straight through to the sound.

"That's what they get for violating zoning laws," said Dan. "If they hadn't put rental apartments on ground level, they wouldn't be in this fix. Storm surge has no respect for real estate. Only way to build at a beach is up on stilts. Water can push through without resistance." He drove over Banks Channel bridge and turned right toward the Club. Piers and docks were twisted off pilings, boat masts protruded from the water, large chunks of debris floated on the outgoing tide. A National Guard vehicle passed by, manned by six armed Guardsmen.

"Why do they need their rifles?" asked Windham. "This place is numb with shock. Nobody's going to create a ruckus."

"Looters," said Dan. "Swoop in after national disasters, burglarize homes, make off with other people's boats and trailers. Guardsmen are only window-dressing, to maintain order. Not going to shoot anyone."

He parked the car in front of the old McInnes cottage. Wood shingles and broken lattice were strewn across marsh grass left by storm surge. "This is our family's place," Dan said. "Though we don't use it much any more. Nora's boycotting because I won't put in air-conditioning, rather have the ceiling fans with their whir-whir-whir. Want me to take you on tour?"

"I'd love it! Our place is all new and contemporary, kind of sterile."

They stepped over a twisted hammock and crab pots as they mounted the stairs to the porch. Horse conchs were heaped against the broken railing. "You've got at least one shell-collector in your family," said Windham.

"My grandmother. As she aged, shells were the only thing which held her interest. She'd use them for soap dishes, put them in lamp bases, hang them on the Christmas tree. If Toby really wanted to please her, he'd find her a sand dollar or a Scotch bonnet, put it in a box as a surprise. Her last request was for conch shells on her grave." Dan jiggled the knob on the back door and kicked it open. "Never have to lock it," he said. Just have to know the right touch."

The house was dark and dank inside. Dan flipped a light switch. "No power," he said. "Follow me. The best is yet to be."

They walked down a long, wide hall panelled in cypress. As they went up the stairs to the second floor, they passed framed photographs coated with salt moisture. An assortment of people stared back at them, holding fishing poles and oars, picnic baskets, beach umbrellas. "McInnes clan," said Dan, "retrospective of the last century."

One photograph caught Windham's eye. A sunburned boy smiled out at her, wearing orange surf jams and holding a green boogie board. "My son Toby," said Dan, "when he was twelve."

She examined the photograph more closely. "Looks just like you. That curly hair, those blue-blue eyes, the silly grin."

"Everybody said Toby was a chip off the McInnes block." Dan pointed to a black-and-white photograph farther up the wall. Another boy stood still for the camera, holding a crab net in one hand and a bucket in the other. "Me, about the same age." He sighed as he climbed to the top of the stairs. Walking on grass matting, he led her past rooms with louvered doors which gave privacy while allowing a flow of air. At the end of the hall, he pushed open a door into a large bedroom decorated in faded flowered chintz. The furniture was wicker, and braided rugs were on the wide floorboards. "My great-grandmother made those rugs. Out of discarded stockings, men's ties. With her own hands. Never threw away anything. A recycler before it became trendy. Ah, the patience of that woman! Patience has been a McInnes trademark. Though Nora calls it procrastination." He hit the heel of his hand against a window sash, pushed the window upward, and secured it with a bamboo stick. Then he unlatched the outside shutters and threw them open to let in air. "See there!"

Windham caught her breath. The vista was magnificent. A long walkway led through dunes out to the wide, white beach, now lined with a thick layer of marsh grass, and beyond the beach the ocean rolled smoothly, innocently, as if it had never violated the land with storm surge. "How can it look so serene, after that raging storm?" asked Windham. You'd think you'd see dead fish, something to mark the hurricane's passing."

"In a day or two, you'll see great heaps of seashells," said Dan, "sucked off the ocean floor. Takes awhile for them to show up. Never understood why." He leaned out the window, gulping air. "This was my room the whole time I was growing up. Every morning I would exhale, to rid myself of the day before. Then I would inhale the beach air, to make me strong for the new day."

Windham gently squeezed his bicep. "It made you strong. You're the man I'd most want to be with on a deserted island."

"I am, am I?" Dan picked her up and carried her to the bed, sank onto it with her, causing it to sag in the middle and the springs to squeak. "This is something I dreamed about when I was in high school, be here with a girl. Never happened. Thank God for second chances." He pushed her sweater above her chest, placed his hand on her breast, began to kiss her.

"Why, Commodore, sir," she said, "you brought me here under false pretenses."

"Did not."

"Did too."

He kissed her again, hard this time, and she gently bit his lip. "Ouch!" He pressed his mouth on hers. "Do it again."

She nibbled at his lips, caught his tongue between herteeth. "Fuck me," she murmured. "Please. If you don't, I'll tell my mama."

"Girls who use dirty words deserve a spanking." He popped her lightly on her bottom. He heard a National Guard vehicle roll past on the beach, and the far-off voices of Guardsmen. "Poor bastards," he said. "If they only knew what they were missing."

As they left the cottage, a small photograph in a dusty frame caught Dan's eye. On the Club pier, a man displayed a basketful of crabs to a small girl. "That's your Uncle Clark," said Dan. "He was a master crabman."

"That's me with him!" squealed Windham. "In 1954, before Hazel. I remember the crabs hanging onto each other trying to climb out of the basket. In the Club kitchen when Uncle Clark dropped them into the big pot of boiling water, they went from blue to pink, and it made me cry because I thought they must be in pain."

Dan picked up the picture so he could examine it more closely. He shook his head. "So you've been here near me all these many years, and I never knew you."

"For everything there is a time and a season," said Windham.

They drove a bit further to the Club and parked soundside. Boats were willy-nilly, resting on each other, turned on their sides, slammed against the docks. Dan stared at the spot where he had hastily moored *Mandamus* as the wind increased to hurricane force. "It's not there," he said. "Damn thing's disappeared."

"I don't believe it," said Windham. "Big boat like that. Where could it go?"

"A million places. Out to sea through the inlet. Down the waterway to a spoil island."

"Maybe it sank." Wiindham ran out onto the dock, which tilted crazily.

Dan went after her. "Get off here," he said sternly. "Dock's badly damaged. You don't want to get tossed into a bed of barnacles."

Windham ignored him, lying on her belly on the dock and staring down into the water. "I don't see anything."

"That's because it ain't here. Like *Minnehaha, Mandamus* is no more."

They heard the sound of a motor, and a jon-boat putted toward the dock. Its skipper waved at them. "Peter!" shouted Windham, waving back.

"I say," said Peter as he fastened the line to the cleat. "What brings you out on such a splendid day?"

"I could ask you the same thing," said Windham.

"I'm looking for exotic species." He bent down into the boat and brought up a coconut. "Found one."

"Mariah must've brought that in from Florida."

"Quite so. Actually, I'm just fossicking about enjoying the destruction of other people's property."

"My goddamn boat's disappeared. I ought to look for it," said Dan.

"How do you propose to do that? Walk on water?"

"Damned if I know."

"Let's try the spoil islands," said Windham as she got into the jon-boat. "Start there."

"If your boat went out to sea in that typhoon, you'll never see her again," said Peter.

"Hurricane," said Windham.

"Climb aboard," invited Peter. "We'll have a go."

"That's kind of you," said Dan, "considering."

"I'm a generous bloke." Peter cast off and started up the motor. As they left the dock, he handed Dan his field glasses. "I'll go slow, and if you spot anything, let me know."

As they putted toward the southern inlet, Dan scoured the marshes for *Mandamus*. Floating docks had surged onto the narrow beaches, and pontoons moved to and fro in the shallow water. Ibis stalked tall grasses, an empty osprey nest clung to a piling. There was no sign of his boat. "Let's take the short cut to the waterway," said Dan. Peter made a sharp right turn into the narrow channel connecting the two bodies of water. "Good thing tide's not out yet, or we'd have a helluva time getting through here," said Dan. A red cooler floated past, followed by an inner tube. The prow of the boat scraped on an oyster bed, and Peter made a slight adjustment to spare the propeller. The channel widened and deepened. Suddenly they were surrounded by porpoises playing tag with each other.

"Look! How beautiful!" squealed Windham. "A big one, and two, three, four...no, six, little ones."

Peter cut the engine as porpoises surrounded the boat, rising and falling, leaping, fearless. Then as quickly as they had come, they disappeared, one by one. "That's the meaning of life," said Peter. "What more can we ask, than to witness such a spectacle?"

"I hate to be a joy-killer," said Dan, "but I'm anxious to locate my boat. Suppose we might motor to Money Island?"

"If you'll direct me."

Dan pointed up the waterway toward a tiny island with a grove of trees at its center. "All the kids around here believe it's where Blackbeard buried his treasure. Always digging for gold coins. But if anybody's found anything, they haven't made an announcement."

A cigarette boat barrelled toward them. As it passed, Dan recognized Jackie Jerrold with Nora at his side, her hair blowing In the wind. They were so wrapped up in each other that they gave the jon-boat no notice. For a moment he felt a pang, seeing his wife in such abandon with such a jerk. "Circle the island," he said to Peter, "while I see what I can see." Minutes later he said, "And all that I can see is the other side of the island. *Mandamus* may be farther down the waterway, toward Hanover Beach. Nothing here except the grove of trees and the giant dune the Corps of Engineers dredged out of the waterway. They suck it off the bottom and spew it out over here, year after year."

Peter headed toward the island and allowed the boat to drift into shallow water. He threw out the anchor and jumped in. "Man overboard!" he shouted.

"Woman overboard!" Windham jumped in after him.

Not to be outdone, Dan held his nose and fell backward into the water. Peter dogpaddled around Windham. "I have an idea," he said. "Want to hike up the dune for a look-see?"

"Nothing behind that dune ridge but a moonscape," said Dan. "Like Las Vegas without the hotels." Peter was already on the beach, shaking salt water out of his hair. "Have it your way," said Dan. "You're the boat captain." The threesome worked their way up the dune, feet sinking deep into the soft sand. When they reached the top, they gazed down into a semi-circular pit. High and dry was *Mandamus,* still intact. "I will be good goddamned," said Dan, sliding down the dune to get to his lost boat. Peter and Windham joined him to check the boat for damage. "How did you know to look here?" Dan asked Peter. "This is unfamiliar territory for you."

Peter pointed toward the right. "Dune is about, oh, nine feet high at its lowest point. High tide and storm surge would be enough to float your boat right through that dip in the dune, and when the water receded, your boat was trapped here, no way out."

"No way out is right," said Dan. "Unless you have a monster helicopter with jaws of steel."

Peter leaned back against the boat's hull. "Or you dig a channel through the dune and wait for a high tide and pull your boat out."

"That's it!" said Windham.

166

"I couldn't possibly manage that sort of monumental task," said Dan.

"I could," Peter said. "With the help of some very good friends on the dredge. Been keeping them supplied with a goodly amount of Foster's, and they've been keeping me company on lonely nights when Windham is with you?"

"Why in hell would you want to help me? I'm stealing your wife."

"I never owned her, so you can't steal her from me," said Peter. "and she's the one who claimed you. I know that much."

"But you're her husband, married to her. Doesn't that make any difference?"

"Tell him," said Peter. "He doesn't understand."

"We're not married like that, in the possessive way, no matter what the law says," explained Windham. "Neither of us is property of the other."

"Years ago we chose to give each other the gift of ourselves," said Peter. "And if Windham now wishes to give herself to someone else, I can't compel her to stay with me. Nor do I wish to, if her heart is elsewhere."

Windham took Peter's hand and kissed it. "You see why I married him? He's the most decent man I know, and he respects me to lead my life as I choose."

"Let's get on with the salvage operation," said Peter. "I'll make my calculations, call in my crew, and we'll deliver your boat to wherever you wish it at the next high tide." He led the way back over the dune to the water's edge.

"The marina on the creek," Dan said. "I'll moor it there while I repair any damage. Of course I'll pay you any expense for the tow."

"You rescued Windham. Turnabout is fair play," said Peter. He pulled anchor as they boarded the jon-boat. "Incidentally," he said, "I'm off to Tibet on Wednesday, for a long stay." He started up the engine. "I'm not that good a husband," he said to Dan. "I go where and when the spirit moves me. Not many wives would understand that."

The boat found the waterway, and they rode back to the Club in silence, sharing the autumn-gold of the marshgrass, the ripple of salt water against the hull. Ibis and herons flew out of the marsh. All was, almost, right with the world.

Greens

When the green warning flag is flown, ocean

conditions are excellent, though swimmers

should take the ordinary precautions.

Rule 21

Fearrington Yacht Club Handbook

Dan lay in the dark aft cabin listening to the clang of the halyard slap the mast in the raw wind which whistled about the shrouds. He disliked living aboard at the marina while he made major repairs. But it seemed the least he could do, allow Nora to remain in their comfortable home while he did his frugal penance for his affair with Windham. Working on the boat all day, most nights he rapidly fell into a deep sleep after a shot or two of Jack Daniels. He didn't bother to change his greasy, sweaty clothes. When he had exhausted himself, he would simply wrap the scratchy woollen blanket around his weary body and rest his head on a life jacket. He hadn't shaved for at least two weeks. His beard was coming in gray with irregular patches of white, and his fingernails were encrusted with layers of fibreglass, paint, and varnish. Doesn't seem much point in cleaning up, he reasoned, living in isolation from his fellow man. He was much too rank to inflict himself on other human beings. Existing as a monk and mortifying himself seemed proper atonement for his sins.

Tonight as he shifted uncomfortably on the berth, inhaling the stench of his unwashed body, he missed the after-buzz of beer and wished he hadn't switched to whiskey. All the way up into his throat he felt burning, a dull ache interspersed with sharp twinges of pain. Could he be getting an ulcer? He'd been subsisting on cold chili from a can, and cup after cup of rancid coffee from the free pot outside the marina office. His daily intake of caffeine, alcohol, and Mexican seasonings might be eating away at the lining of his gut. Since the damage from Mariah caused the berth to slant slightly downward, gravity could be affecting his digestion, a lethal mixture sliding up into his esophagus. He even felt a twinge of nausea, and pain pulsed down the side of his neck through his left shoulder. He had leaned too long over the boat's side wielding his varnish brush. To ease the spasm in his jaw, he opened his mouth as wide as possible, then closed it tight, as if he were the whale swallowing Jonah. Perhaps that was the genesis of his problem, eyes bigger than his stomach. Windham was quite a bit for any man to handle, and he had not been up to the challenge. Her way of life, open and free without regard for social convention, was to be envied. But she had always lived the summer-of-love California way, whereas he was used to Bible-belt Southern convention, stifling his impulses, obeying the law,

172

not making his own rules. Was it unreasonable for him to feel overwhelmed by the sudden rush of fresh air against the tender places where invisible social shackles held him in bondage?

He thought of her face when he informed her he must back off, go to a neutral corner, avoid contact with her. It was the closest she had ever come to crying. They had been gathering seashells from the bounty dredged up by the late-season hurricane. When she found a perfect shell, she treated it like a precious gem, washing it in sea water and carefully placing it in the pocket of her windbreaker. She particularly liked the olives, with their glassy sheen and smooth torpedo shape, rolling them over in her palm in a sensuous manner which reminded him of her lovemaking. When he was with Windham, the world seemed more alive, filled with sexuality, colors brighter, smells more intense, shapes and textures exciting. He no longer felt like an aging good ole boy, but more like a youth on the cusp of manhood. As they made their way along the tideline, seagulls ran ahead of them, leaving undulating trails of fern-like impressions in the sand. Windham studied the gull prints for a few moments, a look of puzzlement on her face. Then she squealed in delight and began inscribing semi-circles on the lower halves of the prints. "Look!" she said. "The gulls are making peace signs. I knew they reminded me of something, and you see, that's it, the way the Y divides and attaches to the curving edge. It's a peace symbol, if I finish it off."

Thirty years before—could it have been so long ago?—Dan had seen peace logos on longhaired flower children who marched in front of the federal courthouse downtown. Windham was right, gull prints did resemble pairs of peace signs stamped onto the sand. "I assume you joined the Vietnam War protests," he said. "I can't imagine you staying away from that action."

"Of course I did. Though I assume you supported that unholy war."

"Actually, I was neutral, because I had a hostage to fortune, my baby son. I was not eager to see young men sent home to their families in government-issue boxes. But I didn't trouble myself with the politics of it, as you did."

She knelt on the sand and looked up at him. "Now you realize that war was a mistake?"

For the first time, he felt annoyed with her. "Yes," he conceded, "I do." He hesitated before he told her what he'd been trying to find the courage to say, creating his best jury argument, making it sound like a plea for understanding. "I want peace in my own time, on the home front. Perhaps you and I have been a mistake. I need a chance to sort through how I really feel."

Her response surprised him, for he had become used to her taking everything in stride. Her green eyes filled with tears, her mouth trembled. She bent her knees and toes inward, cupped her chin in the palms of her hands, like a little child taking punishment. He immediately regretted his harshness, wanted to wrap her in his arms, carry her off to where Puff the Magic Dragon lived in a land called Hanalei, where nothing else existed except loving her. Instead, he stubbornly put on his stern judicial face, turned away to avoid her silent reproach for the hurt he was inflicting upon her. "See ya," he said as he turned and left her alone on the beach.

But he did not succeed in banishing Windham from his awareness. She was always with him. As he went about his work, he could hear the tinkling wind chimes of her voice. Sometimes he felt wind brush her long hair against his face. Windham. She had been aptly named. Once in the oblivion of sleep he dreamed of her on top of him in the fore cabin, her disheveled hair flailing his face as she rode him like a dolphin, rising and falling, almost leaping, falling

175

again, until he rode with her, in the radiance of sunlight which converged on them through salt crystals encrusting the cabin windows. When he came into her, she dissolved into a long, slow wave which propelled him onto a wide beach. All around, above and below, the green gel of seawater the color of her eyes. His orgasm momentarily wakened him and, uncertain where he was, he fell back asleep, seminal fluid wet on his thighs and abdomen, soaking into the wool blanket already dank with sweat. He was again a pubescent youth in nocturnal emission, except that he had no need for anonymous images of generic breasts and cunts, for the object of his desire was specific, and he knew her name.

Sleepless in the cabin, Dan sensed a change of atmosphere. The temperature was on the rise. Bathed in sweat, he threw off the blanket and sat upright to relieve the gnawing pain in his chest. Perhaps he had gallstones. He'd never experienced them, but he understood from Clark Doubeck they could make a man miserable, especially when he had been eating improperly. He fished a chili can out of the trash, flipped on the light, and tried to read the label to determine the ingredients. But the words and numbers were in fine print and without his glasses, he couldn't make them out. He tossed the can back into the cardboard box filled with debris, dug through his emergency kit to retrieve a packet of Alka-Seltzer. Sprinkling the powder on the back of his tongue, he forced himself to swallow the bitter medicine and washed it down with a mouthful of Jack Daniels, praying the alcohol would spare the lining of his gut. Stupid Dan, he chided himself, are you a masochist, following insult with injury?

He hauled himself through the hatch to catch a breath of air. The German words stille nacht came to him as he looked out over the silent boatyard. With the wind down, the clanging and creaking had ceased, and boats rested easily in their slips. Three slips down, a large sloop was decorated with triangular strings of green lights forming the Star of David. The boat belonged to a Jewish dentist, Sol something-or-other-Stein, who sailed on weekends with a shapely young woman Dan took to be his trophy wife. Two weeks earlier, Dan had watched the boat maneuver into the Intracoastal Waterway to join the lineup in the annual holiday flotilla sponsored by the beach chamber of commerce. He couldn't figure out why a Jew would want to participate in a celebration of Jesus' birth. Perhaps the five hundred dollar first prize was sufficient incentive, though the decorations had cost more than this. Instantly he hated himself for his knee-jerk bias. Damn him, he was racist, anti-Semitic to be precise, courtesy of his upbringing. To his new way of thinking, this was reprehensible. He resolved to lend a hand to the dentist the next time he saw him grinding hull blisters. He would become a better neighbor to his boatyard comrades.

He removed his windbreaker and folded it to make a pillow so he could lie back and look up at the stars. The windbreaker was a poor substitute for the Navy-issue sweater he usually kept aboard. It had somehow disappeared during the hurricane. In the chaos of his marital disestablishment, he had yet to replace it, feeling he should deprive himself of new purchases until he and Nora worked out separation of their finances. The sky was perfectly clear. He could see the Milky Way, Orion, Sirius. He wished he had completed repairs and Windham were there, sailing thirty miles out where they couldn't see the mainland, alone together in the vast universe of sea and sky. A shooting star arced its trail and faded out of sight. Dammit, he couldn't get Windham out of his mind. Loneliness was causing him to obsess. Everyone who lived aboard at the boatyard had gone off somewhere else for the holidays, to visit grandchildren or a ski resort or tax haven in the Caymans. Not a soul remained for him to pass the time with. He would clean himself up, go someplace where he could reconnect with other humans for awhile.

Below deck, he did a cold wash to remove the most offensive grime from his body, doused his hair in fresh water, ran a battery-operated razor over his stubble of beard but gave up the effort because the blades had rusted. A faded flannel shirt and pair of worn khakis had evaded hurricane abuse. He quickly pulled them on, eager to abandon his monk's cell and escape to the land of the living. He stuffed a few bills in his pocket in case he needed a tank of gas to make a run to Myrtle Beach where neon signs always glowed OPEN to entice conventions of truck drivers and lawyers and doctors and CPAs who wanted to play a tax-deductible round of golf and flirt with bored housewives seeking dance partners in the famous shag halls. As he exited the cabin, he saw a glimmer on the floor beneath the companionway. To his amazement, it was the tiny artifact he had brought up from the sunken German sub when he went diving with Windham. How had it survived Mariah? He stuck it in his pocket and disembarked to go to his car.

The clock on the dash read almost eleven as he drove by the mall, where last-minute shoppers were searching for stocking-stuffers. Turning into the nearly-empty parking lot, he intended to visit the electronics department of Sears and lounge in front of the giant television screens while pretending to be considering a purchase. But that ploy seemed desperate, likely to mark him as a lonely guy with no one to go home to. He changed his mind, and out of habit swung onto the familiar parkway which led to his home in Forest Hills. Cars were parked on both sides of the road in front of St. Philip's. Nora would be inside the church, no doubt, wearing her holiday sweater adorned with green ribbon and gold bells, holding her head high in the midst of those who would whisper unChristian gossip about her between Christmas carols and hugs when they passed the peace. He hated passing the peace. Who had programmed that into the worship service? His mind did George Carlin tricks. How exactly, should one pass the peace? By sending a bowl of peas around the church? No redblooded man could pass up a piece, excuse the pun. Was passing the peace like passing gas, offering great relief to the passer but sullying the air of nearby passees? This was one of the newly-mandated rituals designed to make God's-frozen-people more touch-feely, but it made him want to flee outside to gulp fresh air. He did not feel peaceful toward the Fearrington city council which had voted against public bus service to the beach because this might encourage black brethren to enjoy God's ocean alongside their paler counterparts. He did not love the lady on the altar guild who snubbed Windham at the Club oyster roast after word got out about her affair with Dan. The accidental fact that these people also attended St. Philip's did not inspire him to want to make nice. He would be damned if he would shake their hands during hypocritical peace-passing.

He shouldn't leave Nora alone on the first Christmas Eve in thirty-five years they had not attended the midnight service together. Impulsively, he squeezed his car into a vacant spot between a Volvo and an SUV and entered St. Philip's through a side door. Making his way up the right aisle, he spotted Nora in her usual place in the second pew from the front, just beneath the pulpit, which the McInnes family had staked out a century before, but the well-dressed man beside her left no room for Dan. Already the church of his fathers was shunning him. As he turned toward the back of the church, an elderly couple in the fourth pew moved closer together and beckoned for him to join them. He nodded in apology for his lateness and knelt for a moment, head bowed in contrition, before he took his seat.

The service was in full swing. Candles burned in every nook and cranny, festooned with holly. Poinsettias lined the altar rail. Reverend Bradley was decked out In his best chasuble. The congregation was splendidly dressed in holiday best. The choir was at full muster. The organist injected special energy into the triumphal sounds which vibrated from the huge golden pipes. For a moment, Dan was glad he had come out of his self-imposed exile into the light and warmth of this church, until he remembered his inappropriate attire. He wasn't even wearing socks, which would be obvious to Nora when he knelt in front of her pew at the Communion rail. During the Lessons, Nora whispered to the man next to her, and the man turned his head so Dan could see his profile. Jackie Jerrold! Nora had invited him to Christmas Communion. Dan was outraged. Jackie surely must be atheist, and he had some audacity to make a public appearance in the House of the Lord at this holiest of holy services. Nora surely was losing her mind. It was one thing to flaunt her maverick lover in private and semi-private places, but to bring him into the church where she had said her marriage vows with Dan, well, that was taking revenge too far. Had she no shame?

When the organ struck up the next hymn, Dan stood and sang as loudly as he could in the rasping voice he had acquired during his tenure as a live-aboard. "Oh come all ye faithful," he fairly shouted in the direction of Jackie, hoping Nora would turn and see him witnessing her spectacle. He upped the ante on "joyful and triumphant," but she still did not seem to hear him. What would Reverend Bradley think when he assumed the pulpit to deliver his Christmas sermon, as he surveyed congregants and saw stalwart Nora McInnes in the company of this reprobate who wore an earring? And behind him, vestryman emeritus Dan McInnes alone and unkempt, in garments more suitable for a hunting expedition?

But Reverend Bradley did not claim his place in the pulpit. Instead, he walked to the center aisle and announced, "I take this occasion to present to you the Reverend Joshua James, who has come to St. Philip's from Baltimore to serve as our associate rector. He has graciously agreed to deliver this evening's sermon. Let us welcome him." The congregation nodded affirmation as a black man in priestly garb entered from the sacristy. Heads turned toward each other, and Dan heard muffled intakes of breath. Never in a million years would he have guessed he would see the day when St. Philip's called a black priest to minister to the stuffy parish. What had possessed the vestry? Had the Bishop deemed political correctness the order of the day? How did Reverend Bradley really feel, in his heart of hearts, about sharing his pulpit with a black priest on a regular basis? Taking advantage of the season of good will to introduce Reverend James was a clever ploy indeed. Dan had underestimated the political acumen of Reverend Bradley. For this he got high marks. Dan was glad he had not missed this historic moment. His anger toward Nora and Jackie subsided with each word rolling from the ecclesiastical crow's nest. It was sheer pleasure to witness the affluent white congregation captive to the status and authority of a black priest with his own take on the Christmas story. Reverend James played his role well, his homily articulate but not presumptuous, a bit of fireside chat with discreet touches of humor, winning most parishioners over before they could coalesce against him. Dan was surprised. Joshua James had followed God's call to the priesthood, but he would have served mammon well as a successful trial attorney.

To show his appreciation for the surprise sermon, Dan put all his bills into the collection plate, noticing three twenties had made their way into his pocket when he thought he was only arming himself with fives and tens. When he knelt at the altar rail for Communion, he deliberately hiked his trouser legs high so his bare, unsocked ankles would incite Nora's disapproval. He continued down the aisle after he completed the Eucharist, rather than kneeling politely in the pew until the hundreds of other parishioners had been served. Outside the church, he stood off to the side waiting for Reverend Bradley to wish Merry Christmas to everyone as they exited, Reverend James smiling beside the senior priest. After the crowd had dispersed and Reverend Bradley had entered the parish office, Dan followed him, overwhelmed by a compelling need to make a private confession and ask for absolution for his more recent sins. A telephone was ringing in the downstairs office where the parish secretary usually ran interference. Dan heard the answering machine pick up and parrot the holiday schedule of services. As he mounted the stairs, he heard a toilet flush, a desk drawer open and shut, and a door close. Reverend Bradley appeared startled to see Dan, but he recovered quickly. "Well, well, Dan McInnes," he said heartily. "Good to see you among us again."

"I know you must want to get home to your wife," Dan said, "but I need, that is, I want to talk with you for a moment. Upstairs in private. I know it's an imposition...."

"Certainly." Reverend Bradley locked the outer door and led the way to the upper room. "Actually, my wife is out of town visiting our daughter in Texas. New grandchild. I've nothing but an empty house to go home to. I don't mind atall our having a conversation." He clicked on the porcelain lamp on the mahogany table beside the crewel-upholstered wing chair. "Sit, sit, please."

Dan glanced around the room before he sat down, checking to see whether any recent titles were on the bookshelf, new pictures on the walls. To his surprise he saw on the rector's desk a copy of the book Nora had thrown at him, Losing Malcolm. Had she donated it to St. Philip's? Or did the church have its own copy? Perhaps he should have read it before he moved to *Mandamus*. "That book," he said, pointing, "my wife has that book. I haven't had a chance to read it."

"Good for bereaved mothers," said Reverend Bradley. "We have a discussion group."

"I...we...lost our son," Dan blurted. "But that was a long time ago. Not what I want to talk about with you." He added, "I was on the vestry, used to be in this office at least once a week, commiserating about diocesan directives."

"Before my time," said Reverend Bradley, "but we still commiserate about directives. They seem to have become more numerous." He rummaged through a pile of papers on his desk. "Have you seen the new official position on human sexuality? Over sixty pages."

Dan laughed. "There's a new position for sex? Is it a codicil or addendum to the missionary position?" Codicil. Addendum. There he was again with legal jargon.

Reverend Bradley laughed with him. "Drafted by insurance company lawyers to protect us from lawsuits filed by alleged victims of promiscuous and predatory priests and youth ministers. Lawyers run the church nowadays." He nodded at Dan. "Present company excepted, of course."

The word promiscuous slapped Dan in the face. He might as well get to the heart of the matter. "You could call me a promiscuous judge," he said. "That's why I'm here."

"I didn't mean….," said Reverend Bradley.

"Goddammit," said Dan, "forgive me for taking the Lord's name in vain, but I know I've been doing wrong and I can't seem to do right any more. Wrong feels like right, right feels like wrong. Am I saying it plain enough, or would you like chapter and verse?"

Reverend Bradley leaned forward, clasping his hands. "I can hear your private confession without further preliminaries."

"Might as well get on with it."

Reverend Bradley opened the Book of Common Prayer and gave it to Dan. "You go first, then I answer."

"Bless me," read Dan aloud, "for I have sinned."

"The Lord be in your heart and upon your lips that you may truly and humbly confess your sins. In the Name of the Father, and of the Son, and of the Holy Spirit. Amen."

So easy to obtain exoneration for his misdeeds. The Catholics must be on to something, making a weekly pilgrimage to the confessional booth so they can wipe their slates clean and begin a new tally. Tossing a few coins into the poor-box was a lot cheaper than going to a psychiatrist. Dan continued to read, "I confess to Almighty

188

God, to his Church, and to you, that I have sinned by my own fault in thought, word, and deed, in things done and left undone, especially ____." He stopped at the blank space, unable to sort through on a moment's notice what had been done and left undone. He had done Windham, while not doing Nora. How could he say this to a man of the cloth who undoubtedly had led a spotless life in the eyes of the Creator?

"Especially," Dan began again, searching for some legal phrase which would encompass his entire misbehavior, "especially in the act of adultery with another man's wife." The pejorative words took the romance out of his love affair with Windham and made it salacious. He wished he had let well enough alone, kept the Church out of his personal business.

Reverend Bradley took the prayer book and set it aside. He finessed the lengthy absolution which delineated the hierarchy of Church authority and he said simply, "The Lord has put away all your sins."

"That's it?" asked Dan. "I don't have to do a rosary like the Catholics, say Hail Marys and Our Fathers?"

"Henry the Eighth took care of that exercise," said Reverend Bradley, "when he established the Church of

England before he married Anne Boleyn and cut off her head." He placed his hand on Dan's head as he said, "Go in peace, and pray for me, a sinner."

Dan was mystified. Why should the priest ask for prayers for his own sins? Mightn't he go directly to God for absolution? "I can't pray for you," said Dan, "I'm a lawyer, not a priest. We prosecute or defend, but we don't intercede, and when I retired I gave up making judgments."

"I've given up making judgments, too," said Reverend Bradley, "and please call me Chris." Dan wasn't sure he wanted to erase the line of formality between them. He felt more comfortable relating to the priest role than to the man inside the collar. "Would you like a nip of Scotch before we part?" Reverend Bradley opened the door of a small cabinet behind his desk. "I keep it for special occasions, and this being Christmas Eve...." He unscrewed the cap on the bottle.

Dan was tempted by the mellow aroma of Scotch, though it might awaken the burning in his gut. "Pour me a little to wet my whistle," he said, realizing his inadvertent rhyme. What was happening to him? He'd begun rhyming since Windham made up her poem that foggy day on the beach. Was poetry contagious?

As he and Chris Bradley stood together by the window overlooking the now-empty parking lot, he realized how lonely the rector of St. Philip's must be in the parish house when the staff and volunteers had gone home. He had imagined it would be a relief for a rector to have private time, but instead the office walls seemed to close in and the room a stage set where successive rectors could arrive and depart without leaving a mark on the antique furnishings provided by the church women. "I want to compliment you on the masterful way you introduced our new associate rector," said Dan.

"Coming from a chief judge, that's high praise."

"If you don't mind my being invasive," said Dan, "I'm curious about something."

"Go ahead."

"How do you really feel about a black priest here at St. Philip's? I never took you to be a wild-eyed liberal. Your sermons have occasionally been mildly provocative, but you've stayed away from the racism-sexism-homophobia stuff." He took another swallow of Scotch. "Wisely, I might add, considering the orientation of our parish population." Orientation, population. Rhyming again.

191

Chris tossed back another dose of Scotch. "Thank you Jesus for the Reverend Joshua James! Does that sound sufficiently joyful?"

"It'll be tough going," said Dan, "after the honeymoon phase is over. They'll be meeting in secret to devise a means to rid our parish of Joshua James, and likely of you as well."

"I know!" Chris was gleeful. "I can hardly wait for the brouhaha to begin. At last we shall have some drama at stodgy old St. Philip's, to leaven the same-old bread."

"You must not want to remain here much longer," said Dan. "Have you vested in the Church retirement plan?"

Chris was rueful. "I've been holding out for it, but between you and me, I've reached the point where I'm so bored I'd just as soon get booted out and take my chances on the shrinking market for used Episcopal priests. I can always open a Christian counseling practice and do seminars at Sewanee."

"Don't like that term," said Dan. "Christian counseling. Sounds so fundamentalist, not what Brother Freud had in mind when he promoted the libido and probed the subconscious."

"My wife hasn't been enthusiastic about my wanting to march to a different drummer. We've had a great deal of strife over my desire to leave St. Philip's. She says I'm not considering the investment she's made following me about. Attending ladies' prayer groups, listening to bishops pontificate at Sunday dinners."

"I hadn't thought about the wife thing, always considered priests' wives as privileged, with automatic access to a certain social stratum based on their husbands' recognizance." He was doing it again, legal jargon.

"She's pissed…excuse the vernacular…with me for disrupting her comfort zone. I'm in marital purgatory, sleeping in the guest room. While she's in Texas, I've reclaimed my side of our bed." Chris looked apologetically at Dan. "Hope you don't mind my frankness. I've no one I can really talk with. Kind of thing you don't tell a member of your vestry on the golf course, or unload on your bishop at confirmation."

"I take issue with that last," said Dan. "The inner circle knows the bishop has been sleeping with his secretary for at least ten years."

"True. An act of Christian charity, considering God ran out of charm when he created that dear woman. But the bishop is the bishop and I a mere parish priest. Rank does have its privileges."

"The thing with my wife Nora, it's not her fault. She would have continued with me if I had required it of her. But what's the point, when passion has long fled?"

"Church policy on sexuality has loosened up," said Chris. "But it uses the words exclusive committed relationship. Which precludes seeking solace elsewhere when you're legally married."

"Fuck that!" Dan shocked himself when he slipped into street-talk, but he was fed up with the hypocritical mores of polite, God-fearing society. Windham was right. Sex was about wanting to give and receive love with another person, not about rules and regulations. Laws were designed to exercise authority and control, not to be humane. "I want to rescind my confession," he said. "Do you have a nullification ritual in the prayer book?" Rescind, nullify. Jargon again.

"I'll tell you something, but don't quote me. Go for it! I believe at the judgment seat a compassionate God will understand. Without love, life can be dust in the mouth."

"I have somewhere to go right now," said Dan. "If you

want to share Christmas repast with me tomorrow at the boat yard, I'd be honored to have you aboard. *Mandamus*, fifth slip."

Chris put away the Scotch bottle and wiped out both glasses with a handkerchief. "Get rid of the evidence," he joked, switching off the light. "I appreciate your invitation, but Josh James has asked me to partake with his family after service tomorrow." Dan went outside with Chris and retrieved his own car from the roadside. As he watched Chris's tail-lights disappear, he knew he must go to Windham, beg her forgiveness for his cowardice and callousness, ask her to let him back into her heart. Bless me, Windham, for I have sinned against you, be with me now and at the hour of my death, amen.

Following the maze of narrow streets leading to Windham's residence, Dan was dismayed to realize he had been taking her for granted, assuming she had put her life on hold until he made up his mind to reclaim her. Why should she stay in Fearrington during the holidays, with only her Uncle Clark for company. She might have flown to wherever Peter was to effect a reconciliation, or, more likely, share Feliz Navidad with migrants up in pickle country, glad to be rid of an aging good ole boy who would neither fish nor cut bait. The more he thought about it, the more he was convinced he would find her house dark, or worse, a For Sale sign at the curb. He had hardly noticed the pain in his gut during his visit to St. Philip's, but now it bore down again. He shouldn't have accepted the Scotch. If he found Windham at home, his acid stomach would cramp his lovemaking, and if she weren't at home, where could he go to console himself? What if he never saw her again? She had every right to put him out of her life forever, considering his abandonment of her.

When he turned down her street, to his relief he saw her four-runner parked in her drive and lights on in her kitchen. He parked around the corner and walked through her back yard to her kitchen door. But before he could give his signature knock, he heard her telephone ring. Irrationally, he wondered whether a neighbor might be calling to warn her a shabbily-dressed man was on her premises. It occurred to him Peter might be calling from across the world to wish her Merry Christmas, and he hadn't any business disrupting their connubial chat. He started to leave, but he needed to see her face, make a reality check to assure himself she actually existed. He stepped into the camellia bushes and peered through the kitchen window.

Windham was cradling the phone on her shoulder, so her hands would be free to continue whatever she had been doing before it rang. As she talked, she worked something on the counter, pushed it, pulled it, rolled it, patted it, brushed a strand of her hair out of her eyes with the back of her hand. When he saw the white residue on her hair, Dan knew she was engaging in her favorite form of self-therapy, baking bread. He yearned to smell the rising yeast, feel the rush of warmth when she opened the oven door. But her phone conversation went on and on. He could not catch her words and found himself trying to read her lips. I'm a peeping tom, he thought, I should be ashamed of myself. I'm not Santa Claus. She seems at peace with herself. Pass the peace. Pax vobiscum. Who am I to be knocking at her door?

He decided to find a pay phone and call when she hung up, test the waters, whether she'd welcome this sailor home from the sea, or say go screw yourself. The phone on the island side of the bridge was out of order. When he found a working phone at the Fast-Mart on the mainland, he discovered his pockets were empty. He scoured the inside of his car for any coins which might add up to the twenty-five cents he needed, digging a dirty dime from beneath the passenger seat. Scanning the asphalt around the phone booth, he found a nickel and three pennies. Still a dime short, he got back into his car and drove aimlessly, grateful his gas tank still registered an eighth full. When he reached the shopping mall on the wrong side of town, he pulled into a parking space at the deserted Burger King, locked his car doors, reclined his seat, and closed his eyes, inviting sleep to come.

The rising sun woke him. For a moment he didn't know where he was. On his windshield a leaflet flapped in the mild breeze. Retrieving it, he read Celebrate New Year's Eve at Pappy Dick's with the Hot Nuts. He wadded up the flyer and dropped it on the floorboard. New Year's Eve. Again. He hated participating in forced gaiety simply because the calendar dictated everyone should be happy. He would rather get Chinese take-out and settle down with a John Grisham novel, than pay a cover charge for the privilege of kissing a bad-breathed stranger at the stroke of midnight. But first he must get through the limbo between Christmas and New Year's. If he had grandchildren, he could teach them to ride new tricycles, help assemble train sets, take them to visit the Marine Science Center to peer inside the shark tank. He envied people with grandchildren. Perhaps grandchildren would have provided a common interest to serve as glue to keep him bonded with Nora.

He was feeling sorry for himself. How many times had he lectured miscreants in his courtroom not to whine about their plight, but show a willingness to do the time for their crimes and bless taxpayers for providing three hots and a cot rather than lining them up against a wall and shooting them. Life is tough. Laugh and the world laughs with you, cry and you cry alone. The annoying thing about clichés is that they usually are true. If he was determined to be miserable, he might as well go where his low spirits would burden no one. He would pay a visit to the dead McInneses at the moss-festooned cemetery, apologize to Toby for being such a lousy skipper that he sacrificed his only-begotten son to a fickle sea. He would apologize to his father and grandfather for being the weak link in the long chain of unbroken marriages, for besmirching the McInnes name.

He took a shortcut down the paved alley running behind the Wal-Mart store. Beside a dumpster he saw a row of discarded poinsettias in silver foil pots, leftovers which had failed to meet the standards of last-minute shoppers. Taking a leaf from Nora's book, he decided to claim this private property, which wouldn't exactly be shoplifting since the plants were no longer on store property, but would still be, under the law, theft. He chose the best of the plants, the ones with the brightest red and pinkest pink and whitest white, more than thirty in all, and piled them onto his back and front seats. The more he stole, the more he wanted to steal, for he kept thinking of more dead McInneses who deserved this token holiday remembrance. As he absconded in his rolling hothouse, he salved his conscience with the thought that the discarded plants would have done no one any good, and he was saving some overworked underpaid garbage man the task of toting them to landfill.

By the time he reached the closed gates of the cemetery, the sun was making early morning shadows across the road. He got out and pushed on the gates, but they were locked. The cemetery office was deserted, gravedigger's equipment unattended. The only sound was the sighing of the breeze in the moss-laden oaks. Apparently even the death industry took a holiday at Christmas. He turned his car around, feeling foolish in the midst of the plants. Where could he get rid of them? If a suspicious cop stopped him, how would he explain his sudden penchant for poinsettias? Remembering the giant dumpster at the nearby welfare housing project, he headed for it, lowering his car windows to get rid of the cloying stench of the potted plants.

From up the street, around the corner, he heard a drumming, a beating, a jingling and a jangling, a boom-de-boom, the sounds of marching feet, tooting horns, singing and laughter. A parade was headed for him, a rag-taggle line of black people wearing strange outfits, carrying oddly-shaped objects from which emanated raucous music. Some marchers wore headdresses and animal masks resembling wolves and alligators and giant birds. They tossed hard candies and coins to smiling children who ran alongside them. Their leader was a tall, lanky black man in a parrot-green calico cloak which likely had once served as a bed quilt. The man's legs were so long he appeared to be walking on stilts, and his dreadlocks were braided with ribbons and bells. When he pranced, feathers flew from his headdress and floated on the morning air. "Hah, low, here we go!" the marchers sang. "Hah, low, kooners comin', ho rang du rango, juba O, juba O!"

Dan pulled his car off the street and parked by the curb to make room for the parade. When a laughing boy pointed a finger at him, heads turned in his direction, and Dan felt a shiver of fear. What was a white man doing in a black neighborhood on Christmas morning? Obviously, he wasn't Santa Claus and his car wasn't a sleigh. Might they be profiling him as a racist spy for the KKK, or a bondsman out to nab a bail-jumper? Realizing he was sitting inside his rolling hothouse surrounded by poinsettias, he laughed back at the boy, opened the car door, and held out one of the potted plants. The boy backed away, misunderstanding the gesture, but a younger girl gleefully ran up to take the poinsettia off his hands. He brought out more of the plants, giving them to the merry children who held them on top of their heads like water jugs as they marched down the street. In only a few moments he was free of his loot. The curious parade was moving away from him, and he still didn't know what it signified. He locked his car and began following the marchers, feeling a lightness of spirit he hadn't felt in many weeks. Walking in step with a large black woman, he asked, "What's this parade all about?"

Breathlessly she said, "Jonkannu!"

He knew about jon-boats but had never heard of a jon-canoe and couldn't figure out what boats had to do with a street parade at Christmas. "John-canoe," he repeated after her, causing her to shake her head and gesticulate toward her fellow marchers.

"Kooners! Kooners!" she shouted, laughing.

Cooners. These were Cooners, whatever that might be. He never expected black people to use the word coon in reference to themselves, for it was a derogatory term used by whites as an alternative to the word nigger. Was this some sort of black power ploy, embracing the insult as their own to diminish its sting, the way hard-core feminists co-opted the word bitch and made it a compliment. What a curious group of people around him, in their costumes and masks, making noise with home-made instruments. They must consider him crazy to march alongside them, but he had nowhere else to go, and he was having fun.

The marchers seemed to be walking in rhythm, in some sort of dance step as moved along the street. He looked down at his feet, hoping to mimic the pattern. Left foot, right foot, hop and jump, right foot, left foot, hop and jump. Suddenly there it was, a stray quarter lying on the asphalt, unclaimed, just what he had needed the night before to place a call to Windham. He bent forward and snatched it up, folded it into his palm as he caught the rhythm of the marchers. He felt he should give this to some poor child who needed it worse than he did, but he was unable to perform this simple act of charity. Spying a phone booth on the corner, in front of a concrete block mom-n-pop store notorious as a gathering place for drug dealers, he ran to the booth, popped in the quarter, and called Windham's number, praying she would answer. When he heard her sleepy voice, he wasted no time on niceties. "We're having a come-as-you-are party," he said, "at the corner of Eighth and Harrison. Get your lovely butt over here fast as you can, and don't take time to fix yourself up. I haven't shaved and haven't bathed and look like hell. But I love you. Come now. Please. Please. Please please please."

"Give me ten minutes," said Windham, "fifteen if there's traffic." She hung up on him.

The parade had left him, disappearing up the street. But he didn't care. His days and nights of wandering alone in the wilderness were at an end, and he knew beyond a reasonable doubt—there it was again, legal jargon—what he wanted to do, must do, or die trying. He must sign over to Nora every financial asset she wanted, without complaint, give her the Club membership, his judicial pension, say goodbye to the marriage which had outlived its raison de etre, free himself to make a commitment to Windham and free her from a passionless existence with globe-trotting Peter. He prayed his life would be longer than that of the McInneses who had gone on before him.

Waiting for Windham in front of the cement-block convenience store, he began to fantasize about taking her to *Mandamus* and making love to her, living aboard, sailing away to some place where neither of them had ever been, far from Fearrington, from all things familiar, begin again. He knew she would come to him, for he had heard no hesitancy in her voice, flowing toward him strong and sure. In a few minutes, as he scuffed his feet in the dingy, weed-choked strip of dirt bordering the curb, counting empty bottles of Ripple and discarded cocaine packets, he heard her four-runner zoom up beside him. She jumped out of the vehicle wearing what she had on the night before in her kitchen, unbrushed hair free of its ponytail.

He kissed her hard as he could, pulled her tight against him. He took her car keys from her hand and helped her into the passenger seat, got into the driver's seat and started the engine, steering with his left hand while he held onto Windham with his right hand. When they caught up with the parade, he parked the four-runner, and they ran hand-in-hand after the marchers. As he ran he made nonsensical words, John-canoe, kooners, hah-lo, juba-O, juba-O. Windham mimicked him. The parade reached the dead end at the poor-white-trash side of the fenced cemetery. Dead end, that's appropriate, he thought.

Marchers broke ranks, removed their animal masks, and began to socialize. Young men in baggy pants high-fived each other. Older men shuffled about as women set out food and drink on piles of bricks which had tumbled from the poorly-maintained cemetery wall. Musicians heaped their strange instruments in a pile and clapped their hands as the tall man in the calico cloak flung his long legs into the air. The young men performed a street dance which combined moon-walking with an endurance contest, as copy-cat children cheered them on.

Scanning the dark-skinned faces, Dan began to recognize people he knew, a woman who drove a city bus, a magistrate from the courthouse whose name he had forgotten. The magistrate caught Dan's eye and gave him a hard look, taking in Dan's rumpled clothing and the unkempt woman who held his hand, reconciling this image with the dignified robed judge who presided over the "big" court. Resolutely, Dan moved closer to the magistrate and leaned over to speak with him. "Greetings, Judge," the magistrate said.

Dan felt grateful to receive this sign of acceptance into the all-black gathering, and the magistrate's name came back to him. "This is Judge Henry Alston," he said to Windham. "Judge, I'm pleased to introduce you to my

friend Windham Doubeck. She recently moved to town."
Henry Alston and Windham shook hands. "We're both at
loose ends this Christmas," said Dan, "and we wanted to
join in the fun."

"Yes, yes," said Henry. "I wouldn't miss this for the
world."

"What exactly is going on?" asked Dan, laughing self-
consciously. "I never knew this sort of thing took place in
Fearrington. How long has it been taking place?"

"Judge McInnes, you white folk got a lot to learn 'bout
us black folk. We been studying you for a long time, know
more 'bout you than you know 'bout us."

"I've been trying to tell him that," said Windham.

"This here is the Johnkankus celebration, we call it
Jonkannu. Used to be a slave tradition, way for black folk
to put joy in our lives while our masters up at the big house
open their pretty Santy-Claus."

"How come I never heard about it? I grew up near here,
over on Chestnut Street."

"Always been going on in the Islands. A big thing
there." Henry smiled at Windham. "Black folk don't just

207

come from Africa. We also from West Indies. Here in this country, the South, Jonkannu died out for awhile. During the civil rights movement, we black folk tried to look like you white folk, didn't want to look like fools parading down the street in rags."

The tall man in the calico coat shimmied and shook in front of Henry, making it clear they were friends. Windham stepped away from Dan and danced with the tall man, shimmying in what appeared to be a modification of a boogie. The crowd gathered around them. "That's Kooner-John," said Henry. "King of our festivities. Our high priest. A great honor to be chosen."

"It's fascinating about the—what do you call it?— Johnkankus," said Dan. "Reminds me of Mardi Gras in New Orleans."

Henry watched Windham's spirited performance. "After we got over the white-is-right syndrome, straightening and bleaching our hair, wearing tight collars and shoes, we started to appreciate who we are, and rediscovered some of our rituals. More and more young people showing up for it. Gladdens our hearts. Takes them away from the other action, drug-pushers thick as horseflies on a tethered dog.

Pleased you decided to join us. Hope you come again next year. Your lady-friend is also welcome."

"We'll wear masks," said Windham. Dan nodded assent.

As Dan moved in her direction, he tripped over something lying on the ground, a short length of copper wire. Working both ends at once, he shaped it into a circle, and fished out of his pocket the small submarine artifact he had found on his ocean dive with Windham. Working the piece onto the wire, he wrapped the ends and formed a necklace with the artifact as pendant. "Close your eyes," he said to Windham, slipping the necklace over her head. He placed her hand on the pendant. "Now open your eyes." Windham smiled when she recognized the artifact. "You got any money on you?" asked Dan.

"So that's why you wanted me here," said Windham. "You're broke." She took a five dollar bill from her pocket and gave it to him.

Dan folded the bill lengthwise and tucked it into Kooner-John's palm as he stretched upward to whisper in the man's ear. Kooner-John smiled broadly. Dan turned to Windham. "He's the high priest here. Going to betroth us. Now."

209

"You've lost your ever-lovin' mind."

"Yes."

"We hardly know each other. Neither of us is legally free."

Dan turned to Kooner-John. "Please begin the ceremony."

Marchers gathered around as Kooner-John said strange words in sing-song, spread his arms and turned his palms outward, splaying long fingers. His rings sparkled in the sun, and tiny bells jingled. When Kooner-John placed his large palms on top of their heads, Dan felt a rush of energy flow downward through his body, as if he had been touched by electrical current. The surge seemed to connect with similar energy in Windham, who jumped slightly. With a shout, Kooner-John began chanting, "Hah, low, here we go, ho ran du rango, Christmas come but once a year, everybody have a share, juba O juba O!"

Musicians picked up their instruments and people started rhythmically stomping. Dan and Windham crab-walked away, waving as the children threw pebbles. Dan pulled Windham toward her four-runner, saying, "Let's get out of here before they arrest us for false pretenses." They made a wedding caravan of their two vehicles, Dan leading the way to the boat yard. "What an unholy mess," Windham said as she entered the cabin. She poked at the empty chili cans and beer bottles. "I'm surprised you're still able to navigate, living off this junk."

"I had indigestion, but now I know it was really heartache."

She inserted her hand inside his shirt. "Poor baby." She unbuttoned his shirt and tenderly kissed the center of his chest, murmuring, "Let me make you well."

"I'm putrid," said Dan. "need a bath."

"So take a bath, sailor-boy."

"No hot water."

"I'm mama-cat and you're my kitten and I'll lick you clean." Meowing, Windham kicked aside the litter and pushed him toward the fore-cabin. Dan protested mildly, wanting not to inflict his rankness upon her, yet feeling such body-hunger that he welcomed her attentions. If Windham were Nora, he thought, she would be more focused on disinfecting him and the cabin than on making love. Windham's primal lust for him despite his loathsomeness stimulated his dormant sexuality, and he experienced an erection he hadn't known since he was a horny seventeen. He fell onto the berth with Windham, who smelled faintly of the bread dough she had been baking the evening before.

When she tossed her clothing aside, he could see soft tendrils of underarm hair, damp with sweat. After removing Dan's shirt and pants, she arranged him on the bed so she could inspect every inch of him. He heard the wind strike up, and *Mandamus* began to gently rock. "For Chrissake," he moaned, closing his eyes so he wouldn't fixate on his hard penis. "Do it, please," he said, "get on it now, while I've something to make you happy."

She placed her fingertips over his mouth. "Shhh, you have some dreadful cuts and tears on your arms and legs which need immediate care."

He spoke against her fingers, "I have a lot more than that which needs care."

"I see," she said. "I'll get around to it. Around to it and over it and under it and…"

He felt himself grow harder. "Stop teasing me."

"Do you still have your emergency medical kit?

"Somewhere, yeah, dammit, Windham, first things first."

"Exactly." She hopped off the bed and headed for the galley, her bottom wriggling like the first time he laid eyes on her. He heard her rummaging in the cabinet.

"To the left," he said, "behind the bucket of rags."

She returned holding the rusty med kit, which had popped open. "Alum," she said, laying out the supplies on his abdomen, "quinine, aspirin, bacitracin, antihistamine, analgesic, lomotil, merthiolate. Aloe! That's what I was looking for."

"A moment ago, I was thinking how different you are from Nora, but here you are, wanting to fix me up before you have your way with me. What is it with women?"

Windham opened the bottle of aloe. "Sweet thing, it's called nurturing. Instinctive. Goes with our mammary glands, even when we've never borne a child." She stroked the aloe over her breasts so the nipples glistened.

"What are you trying to do, torture me?"

"You deserve some punishment for ignoring me the last couple of weeks." Unrolling the gauze, she wrapped it around his left wrist, pulled his arm over his head and tied it to a portside fitting. She tied the other wrist starboard. "I got you, Sailor-boy." She tied his ankles together.

Dan pretended to struggle free. "You call this nurturing?"

"I'll be gentle." She massaged the soles of his feet with aloe as she viewed his penis, which was still erect. "Beautiful thing," she said.

"Just an old guy's dick."

She stroked the aloe between his toes, began pulling on his big toes as if she were milking cow teats. The squishing sound of the aloe made him wish he were inside her. She traced his foot arches, ankles, calves, thighs. Warming the aloe in her palms, she cupped his testicles in her hands. "You bad bad boy," she said, "letting me be lonely such a long time. If you don't say sorry, I'll leave right now."

Dan's voice was a hoarse whisper. "Sorry. Forgive me. Oh god, please forgive me." Windham climbed astride him and matched her palms to his outstretched palms. He felt the weight of her hips as they rocked with the rhythm of the boat. Her head fell forward so her hair tickled his face, then backward so he could see the arch of her throat, the artifact necklace between her breasts. "I love you," he said, "I love you, I love you."

Afterwards, Windham lay on top of him, her ear pressed to his sternum. "I hear your heart beating," she said, "boom-de-boom, boom-de-boom." She rolled beside him.

"Untie me, please," said Dan. "I want to hold you." When she complied, he wrapped his arms and legs around her so his detumescing penis fitted against the crevice in her buttocks. "If I were younger, I'd do you again." He drifted off to sleep.

When he awoke, daylight was coming through the portholes. Windham sat crosslegged beside him, a paperback book propped open between her legs. "A Farewell to Arms," she said, "found it in the head. Oldie but goodie." She began to read. "'Catherine sat in a chair beside the bed. The door was open into the hall. The wildness was gone and I felt finer than I had ever felt. She asked, now do you believe I love you? Oh, you're lovely, I said. You've got to stay...I'm crazy in love with you.'"

"I'm crazy in love with you," Dan said. "Read more."

Windham turned the pages. "'I loved to take her hair down and she sat on the bed and kept very still, except suddenly she would dip down to kiss me while I was doing it, and I would take out the pins and lay them on the sheet and it would be loose and I would watch her while she kept very still and then take out the last two pins and it would all come down and she would drop her head and we would both be inside of it, and it was the feeling of inside a tent or behind a falls.'"

"Like inside *Mandamus*, the two of us here, the world gone away," said Windham.

"Turn around," he said.

The early morning light illuminated her shoulders and the gentle curve of her back as her voice poured over him. "She had wonderfully beautiful hair and I would lie sometimes and watch her twisting it up in the light that came in the open door and it shone even in the night as the water shines sometimes just before it is really daylight."

Dan twisted Windham's hair into her trademark ponytail. She put down the book and turned to look at him. Tears wet her cheeks. They sat silent for a moment, naked, facing each other, listening to the water lap against the hull of the boat, the sound of seabirds feeding. She patted her belly and the swell of her thighs. "I've packed on a few pounds since you last saw me," she said, "all that bread baking."

"You're beautiful," he said. "I like the fullness of your body. I'll pretend you're carrying my child."

"You're beautiful, too. Don't ever shave again. I like the roughness of your whiskers against my face when you kiss me."

"Nora would hate my chin stubble," he said before he could stop himself.

"I'm not Nora."

"I know." They leaned toward each other so only their mouths touched. He worked his tongue between her lips, loving the taste of her, the softness and wetness. "There it goes again," he said, looking down toward his new erection.

"I know what I want for breakfast," she said.

Clark expertly filleted the large Spanish mackerel and doused it with olive oil and lemon juice before he laid it open on the Club grill. Steam rose from the adjacent grill. "That corn ready to eat?" he asked.

Dan lifted the grill cover and rotated the ears, still in their husks. "Windham has the table set on the dining porch. Brought home-made bread."

"Where'd you come up with corn this time of year?"

"Windham has connections up at Mount Gilead. Migrants look after her. Have a source from south of the border."

"I worry about her working with those migrants," said Clark. "One of 'em might do something to harm her."

"More danger from the field bosses," said Dan. "Hispanics aren't punks. They're working their butts off to support families, doing jobs Americans aren't willing to do."

"Something I've been wanting to say to you for quite a while. Guess now's as good a time as any."

"Fire away. But if you try to make me back off Windham, you can save your breath."

"Fact is," said Clark, "I think you two are meant for each other. Happiest I've seen her since she was a little kid.

Peter's a nice fellow, talented photographer, but something always was missing between them. Seem more like brother and sister than lovers, if you know what I mean."

"Passion," said Dan. "That's the word you're looking for."

"Quite so. Life ain't worth a bucket of warm spit without it." Clark lifted the mackerel off the grill and onto a large white china platter.

Dan placed the ears of corn on a tray. "Help me husk this. Watch out. Hot as the devil." Clark began stripping the charred husks from the steaming ears. "So what do you want to tell me?"

Clark lowered his voice. "I'm gay, Dan. Homosexual. It's time you know."

Dan tried to keep his equilibrium as he stripped corn husks. "Sure fooled me. Best-kept secret at the Club. You've fooled all of the people all of the time." He tossed the husks into the waste bin. "Windham doesn't seem to be aware of it. Thinks you're her bachelor uncle, a rare and free bird, not wanting the shackles of matrimony."

"The usual explanation is he hasn't found the right woman yet," said Clark with a chuckle. "I'm the favorite escort for all the Club widows."

"Why are you telling me?"

"Damn hard to pretend all the time. Once in awhile you want someone to accept you as you really are. I feel I can trust you now. Your attitude's been changing a lot lately. Not as hard-assed as you used to be. You've stopped laughing at the jokes."

"The jokes?"

"Nigger jokes, Jew jokes, bitch jokes, queer jokes. Stock in trade for good ole boys."

Dan lined the corn up in two rows and lifted the tray. "Long as you don't make a pass at me, I'm okay."

"Never been my type."

"Sam St. Clair? Your constant friend. Or do I misperceive?"

"If we walk like ducks and quack like ducks, we're usually ducks, aren't we?" Clark picked up the fish platter.

"A little duckie tells me you've been to the gay church on at least one occasion. Should I read something into that?"

"Yes." Dan accompanied Clark to the dining porch. "It means an old dog can learn new tricks. Like respecting the right of people to fulfill their own destinies without my permission."

Clark pushed opened the screen door and ceremoniously bore the platter of mackerel to the table where Windham and Sam filled mugs with hot coffee. "Bit nippy out tonight," said Sam. "We decided to make up a pot."

"Still winter," said Clark. "Glad we've got the Gulf Stream. Think of the poor suckers up North."

"Lovely camellias," said Sam, touching a blood-red flower in the vase.

"From Windham's yard," said Dan.

"Bread smells delicious."

"From Windham's kitchen."

Clark lifted the lid off a large china bowl. "Sam makes a

mean ratatouille." He stirred the zucchini and tomato concoction.

"I grow my own herbs," said Sam.

"Any problem with cilantro in this climate?" asked Windham. "My basil and rosemary went gangbusters this summer, but cilantro was puny. In California cilantro's a good crop."

"Windowbox gardening," said Sam. "That's the answer. Get to enjoy the aroma and pretty flowers along with the seasonings."

"I'm feeling left out," said Clark.

"Me too," said Dan.

"Let's talk man-talk," said Clark, "like how we snagged the Spanish mackerel."

"Couple of chauvinists," Windham said to Sam. "I'm usually outnumbered with these two guys. Glad you're here to even the score."

Beyond the screened-in dining room, the moon rose full above the ocean and made a shining path over the rolling waves. The foursome ate heartily, slathering butter on the corn, piling cobs in the center of the table, sipping from mugs of steaming coffee. When Windham passed around the key lime pie, Sam took a large piece. "The real thing," he said. "Only place I've been able to get that is Key West. Around here they make it with lemons with green coloring."

"Uncle Clark vacations at Key West every year," said Windham. "But you know that, don't you, Sam?"

Sam glanced at Clark, who nodded his head. "I'm aware of it," said Sam.

"We always travel together," said Clark.

"Of course," said Windham. "Dan and I will be traveling together, when he gets *Mandamus* back in commission."

"Bermuda," said Dan. "Or maybe well sail away for a year and a day, to the land where the bong-tree grows. If my scheme backfires."

Clark was immediately attentive. "What scheme? You know how I love schemes." He winked at Sam.

"For everything there is a season," said Dan.

"Or a seasoning," said Sam.

"As we speak," said Dan, "the new member nominations are being posted for voting. In two weeks, we'll know who we'll be showering with, cooking with, drinking with this season."

"True," said Clark.

"I propose to break the color barrier. With your help."

"My god, Dan," said Windham. "Isn't it bad enough you're involved with me? "They'll tar and feather you if you invite a black person to the Club."

"I don't plan to simply have one to dinner. I mean to put one up for membership."

Clark rocked back and forth in his chair. "And where will you find this test case? Has Jesse Jackson moved to town?"

"If Jesse Jackson became a member of the oldest yacht club in the South, Senator Jesse Helms would turn over in his KKK grave," said Sam. "The two Jesses."

Dan poured himself another cup of coffee. "I've just the right person. Already asked him, and he's willing to be the sacrificial lamb."

"Who, in the name of God?" asked Clark.

"You're getting warm," said Dan. "In the name of God, it's Reverend Joshua James. New associate rector of St. Philip's. Cradle Episcopalian from the lineage of Ham."

"What's your boyfriend talking about?" Clark asked Windham.

"Come on, Clark, you've had your turn at Commodore. You know how the system works," said Dan. "A member can put up his pastor for honorary membership, season by season. Always been done, as a courtesy. You've seen the collars come and go, Episcopalian, Presbyterian, rarely a Methodist."

"Never a Baptist," said Clark.

"Why is that?" asked Sam.

"Baptist is not Fearrington Yacht Club chic. We're a drinking club. Baptists don't drink. Not openly," said Dan. "Billy Graham wouldn't be able to get his foot in the door."

"So it's not just Jews kept out," said Sam. "It's Catholics, Christian Scientists, Mormons, Quakers..."

225

"Don't forget Muslims," said Clark. "What's this about Joshua James?"

"He arrived in Fearrington a couple of months ago. Few people know him. And you have to admit, his name has a certain white aristocratic panache."

"You say he's at St. Philip's. Half our Club members attend church there."

"No, they don't! They belong, but seldom show up. You know how Episcopalians are, Christmas, Easter, weddings and funerals." Windham and Sam laughed. "St. Philip's has been a revolving door for clergy. Priests come and go, and nobody pays much attention. Frankly, the only time I see Reverend Bradley is when I run into him here at the Club. He doesn't cast much of a shadow.

"So you plan to nominate this black pastor...."

"Black priest. That's what Episcopalians call them nowadays, you Godless Presbyterian!"

"Priest sounds mighty Roman to me," said Clark. "Thought your denomination was inching forward into the now, rather than regressing into Anglicanism."

"I'll put him up this season along with renominating Reverend Bradley, and hope he passes muster without too much to-do."

"And if there's to-do? You know how Margaret Monmouth is. That busybody hardly lets a fly land on a fish head without calling a constitutional convention."

"If there's a to-do, that's where you come in," said Dan.

Clark sat straight up in his chair. "Now it's getting interesting."

"You've a lot of chits to call in. In your quiet way, you're the most powerful member of the Club."

Clark patted Sam's shoulder. "You see? Been trying to tell you I'm indispensable."

"I'm serious," said Dan. "Lot of members owe you. Time they pay their unofficial dues."

"What's Dan talking about?" Windham asked Clark.

"Clark Doubeck's kept their names out of the paper, held the police at bay, negotiated truces with ex-wives, financed new boats," said Dan. "He's a power broker.

Best of all, he'd done it behind the scenes, so they don't lose face, sully their family heritage."

"Not to mention pretending I don't recognize them at drag parties out of town," said Dan.

Windham looked at her uncle. "I thought you'd never come out of your closet."

"You knew?"

"Since I was fifteen. I figured it out."

"So you've been covering for me all these years?"

Windham tweaked his earlobe. "You're my favorite funny uncle. Your sexual orientation never mattered to me."

Clark stood up. "Give me five!" He slapped Dan's palm with his palm. "I'm on board with your scheme. Just tell me where and when."

"The day of reckoning will be at the next Board meeting when they officially draw up the new-member roster. Be there, ready to rock 'n roll. How you accomplish the members' compliance is up to you, since the end justifies the means."

"Morning, Judge," said Fleet Captain Ted Lassiter. "Good of you to join us today."

First Commander Harry Gorham echoed the greeting. "Morning, Judge."

"Morning, Ted," said Dan.

"You enjoying being a man of leisure?" asked Third Commander Paul Enworth.

"I'll send you a postcard from Bermuda and let you know."

The door to the Club office banged open and the Purser appeared. "Surprised to see you here, Judge," said Horton Brown. "Thought you had enough of these meetings when you were Commodore."

"Gotta check on you young fellas. Make sure you're keeping the Club on a steady course."

Commodore Watson entered and took his place at the head of the table. The Club Manager presented him with a stack of files. "All here, Sir," he said. "Final tally with number of ayes, number of nays."

"How many made it this year?" asked the Commodore.

"Twenty-two full resident, seventeen full non-resident, five honorary seasonal."

"Sounds about right," said Social Commander Inez Greer.

"Your work's going to be cut out for you," said Paul. "Ladies pushing for a midnight cruise, want new stemware with the Club logo, for their bridge luncheons."

"My wife says you've got to do something about these girls with tattoos," said Ted. "Shouldn't be exposing themselves on the dining porch. Takes away Hilda's appetite."

Horton chuckled. "If they're exposing themselves, that'll whet my appetite."

"Hilda suggests we require them to cover all tattoos. What we'll do about nose and lip piercings, I don't know."

"Why would nice girls want to make themselves look like trash?" asked Paul.

"They're making a statement," said Inez. "Used to be exposing their belly buttons. "Now they've upped the ante."

"Meeting is called to order," said Buddy Watson. "Please read the nominations so we can affirm them. How many voted this year?"

"Pretty good participation. Just under three hundred." The Board members nodded approval as the Manager worked his way down the list. When he called out the name of Sally Gwynn, Inez stopped him. "You mean she made it? Third time she's tried. I thought we had an understanding...."

"She got new support," said Buddy. "Her mother married again. "Did pretty well for herself this time. Husband's the Fleet Captain at the Charleston Yacht Club. Goes a long way with our sailors, entre' at invitational regattas."

"Forget I said anything," said Inez.

The Manager got through the full residents and was halfway through full non-residents when Harry broke in. "Marshall Dockery made it? That sonofabitch still owes me for his root canal. How in hell can he afford the initiation fee?"

"Now Harry, don't mix apples and oranges," said Buddy. "If I blackballed everybody owed me money, we wouldn't need a new parking lot."

The Manager completed the non-resident list. "And with the honoraries, the usual. St. Philip's Episcopal, Fifth Avenue Presbyterian, St. Alban's Episcopal, First Methodist."

"I move we accept the nominations," said Paul. "Let's sign off and post the list and get on with our personal business."

"I second the motion," said Ted.

"All in favor," said Buddy.

"Wait a minute," said Harry. "Something ain't right."

"That's four churches. But we got five honorary seasonals."

"One of them must be old Reverend Chilworth," said Inez. "He could have applied again. Since Mary's death, his children keep him up at the nursing home on the waterway. He's blind now. Can't make it to the Club any more. Just wants to be an honorary to maintain his status. We always indulge him, make an exception to the rules."

"Damned if he could have applied," said Harry. "He's dead. Saw his obit in the paper end of August, first of September, before Mariah hit." He turned to the Manager. "Must've forgotten to put his death notice in the newsletter. Do it next month's issue, with an apology."

"Read out the names of the honoraries," said Buddy. "Maybe we got a miscount."

Dan pushed back his chair. "Excuse me a minute. Too much java for breakfast. Have to take a pi...., excuse me, Inez. With ladies on the Board, I'll have to clean up my language."

"Hell, Dan, don't hand me that crap," said Inez. "I've heard worse on the race committee boat."

Dan went into the sailing office, where Clark sat studying new catalogs. "They noticed Reverend James' name. Shit's about to hit the fan."

Clark assumed a Clint Eastwood stance. "Right on, pahd-nuh, make my day."

When Clark and Dan went into the Board room, the atmosphere was already thick with tension. "Sit down, Judge," said Buddy. "We got us a problem, and looks like you dumped it in our laps."

"May I kibitz?" Clark took a seat.

"Long as you honor our pledge to secrecy in new-member sessions. Only way we can speak our minds," said Buddy.

Ted passed the honorary seasonals roster down to Clark. "Third name on the list, after Reverend Huggins."

Clark put on his reading glasses. "Reverend Joshua James." He glanced at Ted. "So?"

Inez spoke up. "Most members aren't familiar with Mr. James. He's...you know...he's black. That's what he is."

"Seems like the judge would've checked it out before he nominated this man," said Harry. "Especially since Dan's a member of St. Philip's."

Dan chuckled. "You should've known, Harry. Your family's been at St. Philip's for years."

"Dammit, I don't keep up with everything that happens," said Harry.

"You must've missed this year's Christmas service. Reverend James gave a good sermon. Food for thought."

"See here, Judge, if you did this for a joke, it ain't funny," said Paul. "We can't draw attention to this race stuff. May come sooner or later, but we're counting on later."

"I've two rectors at my church," said Dan, "and both of them eligible for Club privileges."

"One of them's a nigger!" said Ted.

Buddy frowned at Ted. "Keep it civil. We instruct our staff not to use that word any more, and we can't have a Board member using it. Not on Club premises."

"You been making a horse's ass out of yourself lately, Judge," said Ted. "Ever since you took up with that legacy member…that Windjammer or Windshear or whatever she calls herself." Harry and Paul snickered.

Clark pounded his fist on the table. "Can't have that. She's my niece. Apologize right now."

"Sorry," said Ted.

"You're going to be mighty sorry if I ever hear you talk ugly about her again," said Clark. "Since you brought up the subject, I am reminded of a certain floozie waitress you got caught with down In Brunswick County. Let's see, what did the sheriff tell me her age was? Jail bait, I think he told you."

"I'm damn sorry," said Ted. "Let's drop it."

"We need to elevate this discussion," said Buddy. "I'm not going to preside over a pissing contest."

"I agree," said Paul. "Question is, does this Club really need this right now? How important can it be to extend privileges to a black man who's never gotten sea-legs? He couldn't possibly compete in our regattas. How could he afford a boat, on a preacher's income?"

"Charlie Jackson doesn't have a boat," said Dan. "Nor does Joe Farnsworth, nor Traynor Robertson. Boat ownership hasn't been a qualification for membership since the Club's founding before the Civil War."

"Strike Joshua James' name," Horton said to the Manager. "I refuse to participate in this charade. When

I'm off the Board you can argue the merits of integration with past-Commodore McInnes. I haven't the patience to deal with him this morning." He glanced at his watch. "I'm a CPA. It's tax season."

"I second the motion to strike James," said Paul. "And accept the remainder of the list."

"All in favor, aye," said Buddy. Dan raised his hand. "What is it now, Judge?"

"Dan's not a voting member of the Board any more," said Horton. "I object to his prolonging this agenda when his voice is now irrelevant."

"I may be irrelevant," said Dan, "but you're highly irregular. Honoraries are automatic. Grave insult to refuse nomination of my church rector."

"Take it any way you want, Judge," said Horton. "If you want to fight a duel, you'll be in the McInnes tradition."

"What's that supposed to mean?" asked Dan.

"In the history books," said Horton. "Your great-grandfather McInnes wounded Olin Lassiter in a gun duel. Meant to kill him for insulting a McInnes guest, but Old Man McInnes was a lousy shot."

Clark stood up. "May I see you, please, Commodore?" He motioned to Buddy to step outside the Board room.

A moment later, Buddy returned without Clark. "We accept all nominations with no objections," he said tersely to the Manager. "I declare this meeting adjourned. Good day, Gentlemen." As he passed Dan, he bent close to his ear. "Why'd you have to do this on my watch, Judge?"

On the way to the parking lot, Dan said to Clark, "What in hell did you say to turn Buddy around?"

"I simply mentioned Sam St. Clair had danced with Buddy Junior at the Christmas soiree put on by Faggots of Old Fearrington."

"Faggots of Old Fearrington! Is there really such an organization?"

"You straight guys will never know for sure, will you?" said Clark. "I dare you to come find out."

"You clever SOB," said Dan. "The Fearrington Yacht Club is now integrated. An historic moment."

"Equity in our time. That's all we gay guys want. Since I just did God a favor, maybe He'll soon let us Club queers out of our closets."

"I hope so," said Dan. "When you're ready, say the word."

"Better prepare yourself," said Clark. "Lot of us here already. Buddy Watson Junior is the tip of the iceberg."

A week later, in the shrimp cocktail line at the New Member Social, Dan introduced Joshua and Mrs. James to Commodore Buddy Watson.

"Call me Josh," said Reverend James.

"Lovely shrimp," said Rosanelle James.

"Can your boat hoist handle a J-27?" Joshua asked the Commodore. "I want to bring mine down from Sag Harbor when the weather warms up."

"Anything you got, we can handle," said Buddy heartily. "Glad to have you on board." He turned to the woman bearing down on his port side. "Want you folks to meet our member with the most longevity, Margaret Monmouth. Margaret, this is Josh James. I'm sure his wife Rosanelle will appreciate an invitation to our first ladies' bridge social." He patted Margaret on her ample arm. "Thank you in advance, Margaret. I can always depend on you."

"Oh, do you cater luncheons also?" Margaret Monmouth asked Rosanelle James as the mountain of shrimp began sliding off her plate.

Josh reached out to take Margaret's elbow to balance her arm. "May I help you to your table?"

"Why certainly," said Margaret, allowing him to take her well-stocked plate. "And please fetch me a glass of tea. Boiled shrimp always make me thirsty." She pointed the way to her table in the center of the dining porch. "Salty, you know. You might consider putting lemon slices on the buffet beside the shrimp, the next time you cater an event. And capers. Yes, capers would be a nice touch."

Josh smiled broadly. "Rosanelle and I are here to learn," he said.

Black

When the black warning flag is flown,

no lifeguard is on duty. Ocean bathing

is ill-advised, and swimmers shall

proceed at their own risk.

Rule 24

Fearrington Yacht Club Handbook

"**M**uchas gracias, Senora," said the wiry Hispanic behind the cash register at La Frontera. He tucked Windham's two-dollar overpayment into his waistband, understanding she meant it to go toward his new baby's christening at the blue concrete Catholic mission on the road which led to the interstate. Beside the cash register, his toddler stared at Windham with large dark eyes.

Behind him, his wife carried the week-old infant in a colourful sling beneath her breasts as she chopped green peppers for salsa. Her long black hair hung straight down the back of her bright pink shirt, and her hips moved in opposition to her shoulders. She crooned to the baby as she worked. "Calia pequino bebe, no diga una palabra...."

Every other day, Windham drove her four-runner the forty miles from Fearrington to Mount Gilead to interview the migrants who picked and packed the cucumbers and peppers which became pickles and relish with the green

243

Mount Gilead Pickle Company label. To meet the increasing demand for low-cost labor, the population of migrants had swelled until their numbers upset the political balance of the small country town. Tensions were growing as demands increased for improved sanitation, housing, affordable medical care, and bilingual education. The prospect of union involvement struck fear in the hearts of company managers. Longtime residents of Mount Gilead became more and more uncomfortable over the fraternizing of their young people with brown-skinned teenagers with hot Latin blood in their veins. And in secret, between agricultural rows, females as young as twelve were being raped by field bosses who held absolute power over them.

Windham's first task had been to establish a presence with the townspeople and the migrants, so she was accepted on both sides. She ate breakfast in the fields with workers, lunched in the Anglo tea room on Center Street, and took early supper at the Mexican restaurant. By becoming a familiar face, she was able to make the connections crucial to accomplishing her objective. "Adios, Senor Ramondino," she said, picking up the six-pack of Chihuahua beer she had purchased as a surprise for Dan. She made her way through the maze of small tables occupied by migrants. Field boss Salvatore Hernandez gave her an admiring glance as she passed.

She set the Chihuahua on the floorboard and hightaiied it out of town, hoping to make it to I-40 before the pickle company went into afternoon shift. She was eager to get back to *Mandamus* and didn't want to be impeded by the slow-moving line of cars on the two-lane connector. Her speedometer indicated 80 as she looked in her rearview mirror to check for law enforcement. Letting out a whoop as she got to the main highway in four minutes flat, she swung onto the overpass, wondering how much progress Dan had made on his last attentions to his boat. Soon sweet April breezes would propel them through the inlet to the ocean. Dan had put aboard a Yeoman electronic navigator and Weather Wizard, along with a new trysail and reverse-osmosis water maker, in anticipation of their Bermuda run. "You only live once," he said, "and it's time to do it up in style." He ordered his sail maker to run up his-and-hers matching windbreakers with *Mandamus* appliquéd on the collars. "Damn corny," he admitted, "like fair-weather sailors. But I have to replace my lost sweater and I want something that brands you as mine."

By the time Windham drove into the outskirts of Fearrington, streaks of purple were showing in the early-evening sky. She stopped to buy toilet paper and dish detergent at the Town-Mart, throwing in a package of tortilla chips to go with the beer. The boatyard was bustling with activity when she arrived, for it was Friday and the out-of-town sailors were preparing for the off-shore regatta. "Dan?" she called as she went aboard. She knew he was somewhere about, for his car was in its usual spot.

He did not answer, and she assumed he was inside the ship's store communing with fellow live-aboards. He had made new friends who did not belong to the Fearrington Yacht Club. A doctor named Shelstein, a couple from Connecticut. She was glad he had company while she was up the road with the migrants, for he was by nature sociable rather than a loner. Far different from Peter, who could charm a roomful of people but preferred his own company and the challenge of foreign travel. The more she got to know Dan, she more she wondered how she and Peter had sustained their partnership for such a long time. Their marriage had been mostly parallel play, he in one corner of the sandbox, she in the other, though their similar appearance made people assume they were bosom buddies. Dan, on the other hand, craved closeness and brought out in her a capacity for intimacy she had never before realized existed.

The galley was dark, which meant Dan had been away from the boat for awhile. She clicked on the light and saw the galley spic and span, no grimy work clothes, no loose tools nor charts. This was unusual, for Dan liked to work all day without cleaning up after himself, put things to rights when she came aboard. Perhaps she should go to the ship's store and alert him she had returned. But first she would change from field clothes to boat clothes. As she entered the forecabin, she stumbled over Dan's shoes. They were on his feet, and he lay face down on the floor, unmoving. "Not funny," she said. "Get up off your lazy ass. Mama cat's home from prowling."

When he didn't answer, she knelt beside him. His legs and arms were stiff and he was not breathing. "Oh god," she said aloud, "oh god, please make him wake up." She climbed onto the dock, shouting for someone to call a doctor. Sol Shelstein emerged from his boat and came running. When he entered the cabin, he turned Dan face up and listened for a heartbeat before telling Windham what she already knew. "Dan's dead," he said. "Nothing I can do." He put his arm around her.

"Not fair," she whispered. "He just finished getting *Mandamus* in shape to sail. We were planning for Bermuda."

247

Sol held her tightly. "Cover him with a blanket and I'll call the rescue squad. I'll wait with you until they come."

"I should let his wife know he's dead."

"His wife? I thought you were his wife, the way he talked about you."

"Sort of," said Windham. "But not legally."

"What's his legal wife's name?"

"Nora."

"He never mentioned her. Call her later, after you've pulled yourself together."

When later came, Windham let the mortuary inform interested parties. She rolled Dan's shirt and pants around his boat shoes and took them back to *Mandamus*, sat on the deck consuming the entire six-pack of Chihuahua. Sol had told her Dan died a quick death from myocardial infarction. He fell over dead shortly after she left in the morning for Mount Gilead, lay on the floor all day until she came home and found him. Dan had what Sol called a clean death, no fuss, no muss, no bother. "We should all be so lucky," Sol said shortly before leaving Windham alone with her grief.

But she did not feel   lucky.   She had never before experienced personal guilt, and it hurt like hell. Global guilt had been her bag. Liberal do-gooder guilt. Save-the-world guilt. The kind of guilt which allows you to make a protest or a donation and go to sleep at night. Personal guilt caused her to hate herself for leaving Dan alone all day long, made her wonder why she hadn't insisted he go to the cardiologist when he complained of recurring chest pains. This guilt blamed her for enabling him to abandon the way of life which had sustained him for so long. He had lost friends when his affair with Windham became known. He had worried over ending his long marriage to Nora. He had worked himself to death on *Mandamus* so he could sail away with her.

She wished she could locate Peter, ask him to return to help her through what lay ahead. But Tibet was not merely a phone call away. He would be difficult to locate. By the time he arrived in Fearrington, Dan's ashes would be scattered in the ocean. The world would go on about its business, not caring that Dan McInnes was no more. She wouldn't spend her time reaching out to Peter. She would spend it getting *Mandamus* ready for its last sail, to the ten-mile reef where she could release the ashes into the sea and have them drift downward to settle on the sandy ocean floor, where mystical, magical fish swam in the quiet. In the morning when the stars disappeared and the sun came up, she would scrub *Mandamus* from bow to stern, polish up its hardware. Tonight she would mourn Dan. Her voice seemed to come from far away. I'm sorry, she said, I'm so goddamn sorry. But she wasn't sorry Dan had loved her. She was glad. The last few months had been the best of her life. She looked up at the stars. Windham Doubeck here, Commodore Sir, awaiting your instructions.

Windham watched the rain drip from the black awning which protected the newly-dug hole in the ground. Aging Club members huddled near each other seeking warmth on the raw March day, avoiding visual contact with the handsome coffin resting on its bier. Spring flowers blanketed the bier, tulips and daffodils, heather, the arrangement marred only by blue and white ribbons streaming toward the scarred earth. Nora made certain the mourners remembered Dan McInnes had been a Fearrington Yacht Club Commodore. Damn Nora. Still married to Dan under the law, she'd refused to honor his wish to be cremated and scattered in the ocean, insisted on burying him at Oakview and forcing upon him the Club seal of respectability. As if reading Windham's mind, Nora leaned toward her and whispered, "I put his rod and reel in his casket. Thought you'd appreciate that."

Reverend Chris Bradley conducted the graveside service. Face sombre, hands clasped, he looked at Nora as he said the words. "In the midst of life we are in death, of whom may we seek for succor, but of Thee, O Lord, who for our sins are justly displeased?" He abruptly stopped, as if he had second thoughts about the prescribed text. He began again, using the alternate text and shifting his gaze to Windham. "Wherefore my heart is glad, and my spirit rejoiceth; my flesh also shall rest in hope. Thou shalt show me the path of life; in thy presence is the fullness of joy,and at thy right hand there is pleasure forevermore."

He bent toward the ground, retrieved a handful of sandy soil, and let it fall upon the coffin. "In sure and certain hope of the resurrection to eternal life through our Lord Jesus Christ, we commend to Almighty God our brother Dan McInnes; and we commit his body to the ground, earth to earth, ashes to ashes, dust to dust. The Lord bless him and keep him, the Lord make his face to shine upon him and be gracious unto him, the Lord lift up his countenance upon him and give him peace. Amen."

Reverend Bradley wiped the traces of soil from his hands and held them out to Nora, who took them into hers. "Thank you," she said. "I hope you understand about not having the service at St. Philip's. Dan had become rather peculiar about going inside the church. Said it gave him claustrophobia."

A smile came onto Reverend Bradley's funeral face. "Curiously, I've begun to feel the same way. All that darkness, formality, hard surfaces. I'd much rather be out here under God's blue sky." He looked past the dripping awning and smiled again. "Correction. Out in the elements."

"The elements," Nora echoed. "That's what Dan liked, to be out in the elements. Before he retired he would say he'd come to hate the confinement, spending the entire day on the judge's bench in that crowded courtroom. Perhaps that's why he had to get out on his sailboat every chance he could. Yes, perhaps that's why he did it. I used to think it was just an excuse to get away from me."

"Now, Nora," soothed Reverend Bradley, noticing mourners drawing closer to the conversation. "Don't be hard on yourself."

"Maybe Dan felt closer to our son on his boat, the last place he and Toby were together." Nora reached out to pull Windham closer to Reverend Bradley. "You've met Windham Doubeck, haven't you? Dan was in love with her. She's very pretty, don't you think?"

Windham heard a murmur among the mourners, who ceased moving toward their cars and turned once again in the direction of the bier. A frown came over the face of Margaret Monmouth. "Well yes," said Reverend Bradley, "Dan did mention her to me. He spoke of her, yes." He put his arm protectively around Nora's shoulders. "Dan was deeply troubled by his behavior, Nora. I hope you understand this. He cared a great deal about you. He was searching his heart, doing a personal inventory...."

"Fiddle faddle," said Nora. "Our marriage died long ago, with our son Toby. You never knew Toby, did you?" She looked at Windham. "Neither of you knew Toby." Taking hold of their hands, Nora drew them through the rain to a grave near the green awning. The tombstone was inscribed Daniel Tobias McInnes IV, born April 11, 1969, died July 4, 1986, by the wind grieved. "Toby and Dan sailed together," she said. "That's how Toby died, sailing. Silly boy, didn't get out of the way fast enough. Boom knocked him into the sea. Only Independence Day race his father ever lost, that one."

"I'm sorry," Reverend Bradley mumbled. "I knew something about it, of course, your loss...."

"Everyone's loss," said Nora. "Toby was the most popular boy in school. His friends took up residence at our house. Ravaged my refrigerator. Thump-thump of their idiotic music. Toby voted class president every year. A natural leader. Would've been a Congressman, that's what I thought. Dan thought Toby'd lead a rock band, have a bunch of groupies, wear his hair in dreadlocks." She sighed and brushed Reverend Bradley's rain-soaked hair back from his forehead, as he winced from the unexpected familiarity. "You see why I had to bury Dan at Oakview, Windham? Now they're together. Dan and Toby. Father and son. Ah, well." She moved toward the black limousine idling curbside. "Please ride with me to the Club for whatever it is Clark Doubeck's put together to honor Dan," she said to Reverend Bradley. "I'm letting Clark handle the wake. When I got Dan put into the ground, my duty ended."

"That's very kind of you," said Reverend Bradley, "but I've my own automobile."

"You ride with me, please," Nora said to Windham. "I'd rather not be alone just now."

Windham looked at her four-runner, washed in the cold rain. "Thank you," she said, "this will be my privilege. But people will talk."

"Let them talk," said Nora. "They'll have even more to talk about when they see me get thoroughly drunk off hot toddies at the Club. I do believe I'm coming down with a dreadful cold. Must stave it off." She sniffled, blew her nose into her handkerchief, straightened her back, and strode toward the limo, nodding left and right at the mourners. "Come! Come!" she said to no one in particular. "Time to celebrate the life of Dan McInnes!"

The rain was a gray veil over Banks Channel by the time the remnants of Dan's funeral procession straggled across the drawbridge. Wind whipped the boats moored in the choppy water. Inside the limousine, Nora and Windham rode silently, faces turned away from each other, staring through port and starboard windows which provided a surreal perspective of the narrow island. Nora could see tasteless new three-story beach houses crowding out the

255

charming, low, weathered cottages nestled among the dunes. The lower windows of the old McInnes cottage were still covered with plywood for protection from Hurricane Mariah. Roof shingles were missing, flung about on the sand below, and lattice had been torn from the long-vacant maid's quarters. For a moment, Nora felt annoyed that Dan had postponed making repairs to the cottage until after he restored his boat to sailing condition. Then she remembered her husband was beyond her reproach, interred at Oakview beneath the Spanish moss draping the oak trees which sheltered McInnes graves from the elements.

As the limo turned past the Club boathouse into the rain-sheeted parking lot, Windham remembered Dan's arms tight around her as they listened to Mariah raging outside. She could still feel the weight of him upon her, hear his heavy breathing as his desire was heightened by the lethal energy of the storm. Her body began to ache for loss of him, and she barely controlled a strong urge to slap Nora, inflict pain upon her for failing to meet the needs of her husband after the death of their son. Windham gripped the velour of the back seat with her fingers until the irrational impulse subsided.

The Club Manager opened Nora's limo door, slipped his arm into hers, and motioned to Windham to take his other arm, as he balanced a large black umbrella which afforded scant cover from the driving rain. After both women were deposited safely beneath the Club's wide eaves, Nora said apologetically, "I've decided to finesse going onto the beach for Clark's event. Catching a cold, I'm afraid. I'll just slip upstairs to the bar and warm myself with toddies, while you pay your respects."

Against the gusts of wind and rain, Windham made her way down the slippery boardwalk and looked out at the angry ocean. She could not find the horizon, could not distinguish shore from sea, sea from sky. Ahead of her, Uncle Clark was affixing a black flag to the left hand corner of the lifeguard stand. He was outlandishly outfitted in a plaid kilt, and as he dismounted, the pleated skirt flapped in the stiff wind. Drenched with rain, Clark winked at his niece on his way back to the Clubhouse. "Ever wonder what a Scotsman wears under his kilt?" He joked in a lame effort to lighten the torment of the day. "This was Dan's McInnes tartan. I don't know what he wore under it, but we gay guys prefer lace on our drawers." He did a poor imitation of a highland fling and danced away from her.

257

Rivulets of water coursed down Windham's cheeks and dribbled into the collar of her slicker as she saw a familiar figure coming toward her on the boardwalk. "Peter!" She shouted in amazement and gratitude. "How in the name of God did you get here from Tibet?"

Peter Arnold seized her shoulders and kissed her with more passion than she had ever known in him. "I couldn't believe it when Geographic forwarded the message from Clark. Even you didn't know I was at the Tsango in Pemako."

That was like Uncle Clark, to work both sides of the street, maintain communication with his niece's lover and with the husband she was cuckolding. Clark's gift for diplomacy allowed him to remain in the gay closet all those decades until he came out to Dan. Club members were so fond of Clark they cooperated in the pretense of his courtship of an assortment of Club spinsters, offered their divorced or widowed relatives for his bachelor escort service. Just when a major civil war threatened to erupt and turn cousin against cousin, son against father, brother against brother, Clark managed to build a bridge over troubled waters. And each time Clark signed onto the guest ledger the never-married Sam St. Clair, members presumed Clark simply enjoyed the occasional company of this debonair non-member who owned the best antique shop in town. Clark's political acumen also worked in favor of Dan's heretical introduction of the black priest into honorary membership accorded members of the clergy.

"Dan McInnes carked it," Peter was saying. "Whoever would have predicted? I was growing quite fond of the fellow, especially admired his good taste in other men's wives."

Windham gave Peter a light punch to his bicep. "Dan's dead. Pau. Out of my life. Can't you leave it alone, especially today?"

Peter threw his arm around Windham. "My dear," he said, "I couldn't blame him for loving you. Nor you for loving him. I thought I made this clear when I took my assignment on the other side of the world, where I wouldn't impede your progress."

Windham began to cry for the first time since she found Dan sprawled on *Mandamus*. "Walk with me to the beach," she whispered. "I need a mainstay to get me through this thing." Peter obliged her, helping her across the sand now mushy with rain water. Other mourners joined them in twos and threes at the tide line where a lacy edge of brown foam was battered by raindrops. The ocean was roaring

259

with waves up to ten feet, white spume trailing off the rolling crests.

Reverend Bradley took his place in the midst of the mourners, pulling the hood of his slicker up over his head. Reverend Joshua James stood beside him. "We are here together," he said, "to honor the passing of a man who had the courage of his convictions." He began speaking more loudly, aware his words were blowing away in the wind. "Dan McInnes was an honorable gentleman, a leader. His humanity caused him to take risks the more timid among us dare not assume." He glanced at Windham. "Dan's presence in our community will be felt for generations to come. And it was here, on this very spot, that he staked himself every fishing season in hope of landing a big one." He again glanced at Windham, and then at Joshua James. "Dan McInnes was patient. He was attentive. And in due time he made his catch."

Sobs went up from Jerianne, who huddled with the four little Eldridges beneath the tarp Bill held over them. In her arms, wrapped snugly in a ditty-bag, was their new offspring, born a month earlier. Jerianne's face was ruddy, and mucus ran from her nostrils. She rocked the baby back and forth as she moaned. Bill's eyes were fixed on his sand-coated topsiders, but Windham saw tears mingling with the rain which dripped off his cheeks. The other mourners also wept, in their own ways, some with hands pressed across their mouths to stifle the noise, others staring sadly out to sea, shoulders shaking with grief. Suddenly an unearthly sound cut through the rain and thirty-knot wind, and Clark appeared in the McInnes kilt, struggling to hold onto a brace of bagpipes. His cheeks puffed as he strained to create a recognizable tune. The mourners were so startled to see Clark Doubeck parading toward them, they began to laugh aloud, Reverend Bradley with them.

Windham thought she recognized a long-forgotten hymn from childhood. She began to hum as bits and pieces came back to her. Words formed on her lips. "I danced in the moon and the stars and the sun," she sang to herself, "and I came down from heaven and I danced on the earth...." She saw Clark moving his feet in time with the music he pumped through the reeds, and she began to move her feet also, singing so others could hear her.

Peter Arnold picked up on the hymn. "I danced for the fishermen, for James and John...they came with me and the dance went on."

Reverend Bradley joined in. "I danced on the Sabbath

and I cured the lame."

Joshua James added the next line, "The holy people said it was a shame."

"Dance, dance, wherever you may be," sang Jerianne as she came out from under the tarp to follow Clark's steps with the bagpipes. Her children gleefully ran after her. "Dance, dance, wherever you may be...I am the Lord of the Dance, said He."

Reverend Bradley danced awkwardly across the sand behind the running children. Peter followed, tugging on Windham's hand. The rain-soaked, wind-whipped mourners fell into line—Sam St. Clair, Sol Shelstein, Harry Gorham, Ted Lassiter, Horton Brown, Inez Greer, Paul Enworth, Buddy Watson bringing up the rear. Reverend Amanda Abingdon ran to catch up with Clark. The strange procession danced up the boardwalk, across the Club porch, toward the ballroom, where the bagpipes echoed a raucous din. Feet clumped up the staircase to the bar, grinding wet sand into the treads. At the top of the steps Nora peered down at the ragtag conga line, as she steadied herself on the banister railing. She was smiling.

Windham heard the lift creak past, the steel-and-glass cube installed to enable aging and infirm members access

262

to the bar. When it jerked to a stop at the upper level, Margaret Monmouth emerged, water dripping from her yellow rain cape, blue hair matted against her forehead. "Sorry about Dan," she said tersely to Windham. "We were all very fond of him." She made her way to Nora, shaking water from her cape.

The double-doors of the bar were bolted shut against the northeaster which blew gusts of rain across the upper porch. Wet clothing was spread over the backs of settees and chairs. After imbibing alcoholic beverages flowing freely in honor of deceased Commodore McInnes, mourners lounged in customary social posture as they reminisced about races won, races lost, races cancelled because of bad weather. Bill Aldridge confided in Ted Lassiter, "Can you believe it? That nigger from Chicago is running for President of our United States! Not even born in America."

Ted glanced uncomfortably around the room. "Not now," he said. "Not here. Not today. We got Joshua James among us."

Arranging Nora on a settee where she would be in no danger of injuring herself if she passed out from heavily-laced toddies, Clark rapped loudly on the glass cabinet which held sailing trophies. The room hushed as mourners turned in his direction. "I am pleased to announce that a new Cup will be in competition this season," he said. "The McInnes Cup, at this very moment being engraved. We gratefully receive this Cup through the generosity of Dan's widow Nora, who has donated it in memory of Dan and their son Toby." Jerianne prodded Nora, who lifted one hand and waved slowly at those assembled. Clark opened the trophy cabinet with a key and indicated a space between the huge, gleaming Lassiter Cup and the smaller but more ornate Dubose Cup. "Here the McInnes Cup will repose," he said, "offering a great new challenge for our yachtsmen." He re-locked the cabinet.

Bill Aldridge made another run at the bar and returned with a glass full of gin. "I offer a toast in memory of Dan McInnes!" He held his glass high. "No finer man ever trod the decks of this Club, and he will be sorely missed."

In a corner of the large room, near the stairwell, Windham felt apart from the closely-bonded group. No one had shunned her, not even Mrs. Monmouth, most likely because Nora indicated good manners would be the order of the day, despite Windham having lured Dan from his appointed duty. But Windham knew she was not one of them, not really, despite her paternal dna. She was an

264

outsider from some other place, an occasional guest tolerated for her ancestry, a new and less-than-welcome member courtesy of her lineage. Though Dan had disrupted the Club's long-established equanimity by openly consorting in adultery and breaking the color barrier, he had redeemed himself by falling dead. Windham was another matter. She had played Eve to their Adam, tempted him, brought chaos to their Eden. She would exist as a constant threat to their established order.

Peter Arnold read her depressed spirits. He came to stand tall next to her, sending a message to everyone he was on her side. He reached for her glass, poured something from his glass into hers, and raised both glasses. "I offer a toast to Dan McInnes," he said in his carefully-modulated Down Under accent. "The race was to the swift, and the better man captured the prize." He bowed toward Windham.

The room fell silent as no one other than Clark and Sam shared his toast. Jerianne waddled toward the bar, said something to the barista, and returned with a full bottle of champagne corked with her thumb. She shook the bottle, and the champagne erupted in a geyser which sprayed everyone within ten feet of Jerianne. "A toast to Nora McInnes!" she said. "God bless her, she has steered the course." Grateful for release from awkward silence, mourners offered toasts of their own to Nora, who was so far gone her head seemed about to roll off her shoulders.

Peter steered Windham in the direction of Reverend Bradley. "Vicar looks like he could use a drink," he whispered to her. "I'll fetch it from the bar."

Chris Bradley stood off to himself not far from the stairwell, as if waiting for an opportune moment to make his exit. His wet hair was plastered to his skull, but Windham could see curly tendrils releasing themselves over his ears, which were ruddy from wind and cold. He appeared oddly attractive in the navy-surplus sweater Clark Doubeck loaned him from the lost-and-found bin in the men's locker room. "Hello, Reverend Bradley," Windham said, watching Peter elbow his way up to the bar.

"Call me Chris," the priest responded. "When I don't have on my collar, I'm a regular fellow."

As she drew near Chris, she caught a familiar odor coming from the sweater, where it had absorbed rain water. Sure enough, she saw a catch in the right shoulder and small rip at the elbow. The sweater was Dan's, the one he always pulled on after the sun set and the air grew chill. So that's where it had disappeared to after the hurricane. The damp wool mingled with the essence of Dan, with his sweat and the Hawaiian Tropic he had her rub into the back of his neck to ward off the midday sun. She shivered as she caught her breath.

Chris Bradley touched her arm, almost apologetically. "Are you all right? Must be getting a chill from being out in the elements. Mind if I warm you up?"

Windham almost pulled away, not wanting to make contact with the sweater when it was worn by someone other than Dan. But there was something comforting about again being in the hollow of a man's arm, feeling the pressure of his bicep and tricep. She relaxed into Chris' embrace and became aware of an unfamiliar smell mixed with the lingering smell of Dan. It was the smell of Chris Bradley, and it was not unpleasant. As Peter came toward them, holding his arms straight out in front of him to forge a path through the mourners and keep most of the liquid in the glasses, Chris touched his fingers to the pendant at her neck. "What is this?" he asked. "Seems an odd sort of thing."

"Dan made it for me. I never take it off."

"Sorry," said Chris. "Shouldn't have been so inquisitive."

"Quite all right," said Windham, and it was all right, quite all right, for it allowed her to speak of Dan.

"You don't have to explain," said Chris. "If it's private, you don't have to share it with me."

"Dan found it on a dive. Off a German submarine wreck. First time he took me for an ocean sail on *Mandamus*."

"Unhand my wife!" Peter turned to Windham. "You can never trust a vicar."

At that moment, a loud popping sound came from out on the beach, cutting through the drumming rain. Nora jerked to consciousness, and mourners rushed to oceanfront windows.

"Must be the Club generator," said Peter.

"But the lights are still on," said Chris.

Another popping sound followed the first one. Clark opened the double doors, letting in a gust of wind. Rain blew in over the floor of the bar. Nora staggered to her feet and followed Clark out onto the upper deck, huddling against him beneath the roof. A light flashed over the ocean, then another, along with more popping sounds.

"Well, I'll be goddamned," shouted Clark. "If it isn't Jackie Jerrold, the little sonofabitch, shooting off flares."

At the mention of Jackie's name, Nora came alive. Windham watched her make her way to the porch railing, oblivious to the pelting rain. She shouted into the northeaster, waved her arm at the beach buggy barely visible in the murky darkness. The buggy veered away from the water toward the dunes, and Nora slipped and slid across the slick porch, gripped the railing, and disappeared down the flight of steps, reappearing on the path through sea oats. She stumbled, ran zigzag, arms outstretched, as the buggy mounted the dunes. Attired in a wetsuit, Jackie leaned from behind the steering wheel across the passenger seat and caught Nora with his right arm. He pulled her into the buggy beside him and drove straight into the sea, stopping only when the tires were immersed in the choppy waves.

"Reckless bastard," someone said, witnessing the spectacle.

"There's a brave fellow," said Peter.

"He'll kill Nora," said Bill to Clark. "We should rescue her from that lunatic."

"Leave her be," said Clark, starting back to the well-lit bar. One by one, the sodden mourners followed him.

"I'll be off," said Peter to Windham when they were back inside. He seized her shoulders and kissed her directly on the mouth. "I leave you in the care of the vicar." He nodded at Chris Bradley as he left.

"Odd, isn't it," said Windham as she stroked rainwater from her hair. "When I met Dan, I was all wet, and I'm all wet when I say goodbye to him. Full circle." Tears coursed down her cheeks. "Must be some kind of message in that, but damned if I know what it is."

"I'll drive you back to your car in my car. Believe you left it at the cemetery when you accompanied Nora here?"

Windham was weeping so intensely she could barely respond. "Yes, yes." Chris took her hand and preceded her down the steps. He's a gentleman, she thought. Follows the rules of etiquette. But of course, he's an Episcopal priest. She felt ridiculous, concerning herself with the decorum of a man of the cloth, while Nora disported herself on the beach with a social outcast young enough to be her son. If Dan's spirit was somewhere watching, he'd be laughing at the incongruity. Making a run for Chris's car in the parking lot, Windham again heard

270

the popping sound. Red flares lit up the ocean, bursts of light briefly illuminating sky and water, mocking the sad night. She felt a phantom pain in her right ankle, where the bluefish had bitten her months before. "Would you drive me directly home, please?" she asked as Chris helped her into his car. "My four-runner can wait until morning. Right now all I need are dry clothes and a good cry."

Chris drove into town without burdening her with conversation. She listened to the hypnotic swish of the windshield wipers, sound of tires on asphalt. Somewhere out there dear, stalwart Peter was flying away from this place toward the next place where he would pursue exotic species, on his journey to his elusive Shangri-La. With Dan gone too soon, she also must find that place she could call her own. It was not in Mount Gilead when her work was done, and not in Fearrington, she knew that, but where it might be she hadn't the foggiest. Perhaps she should do mission work with migrants in Texas, or with Haitians. She tilted her head so she could look through the windshield up toward the sky. She saw only darkness. No stars. No moon. "If there were a moon," she said aloud, "I would howl at it."

Chris hit a button on the dash and the passenger window rolled down. "Howl anyway," he said. She stuck her head out the window and let the rain blow against her face. It stung her lips as she opened her mouth and inhaled the raindrops. She exhaled, making a timid sound at first, then howled more loudly as Chris began to howl with her. Their voices became a requiem, rising behind and above them in the night.

CPSIA information can be obtained
at www.ICGtesting.com
Printed in the USA
FFOW03n1300020414
4570FF

9 780615 870151